25/02/07

WINGS OF THE DOVES

Pilot Alan Ingram achieves his dream when he launches an air charter service on the small Scottish island of Heronsay. He meets opposition from his wife Susan and son Daniel, both reluctant to leave their studies in Glasgow. Daughters Clare, a medical student, and Jessica, on a gap year in Australia, are supportive but have problems of their own. Each member of the family is faced with adversity and doubts about the future, plus the puzzle of a long-lost relative.

Books by Sheila Lewis
in the Linford Romance Library:

FOR LOVE OF LUCIA
DESTROY NOT THE DREAM
A PROMISE FOR TOMORROW
KENNY, COME HOME
STARS IN HER EYES
A MAN WITH NOWHERE TO GO
LOVE'S SWEET BLOSSOM
AT THE HEART OF THE ISLE

SHEILA LEWIS

WINGS OF
THE DOVES

Complete and Unabridged

LINFORD
Leicester

First published in Great Britain in 2004

First Linford Edition
published 2006

British Library CIP Data

Lewis, Sheila
    Wings of the doves.—Large print ed.—
Linford romance library
1. Love stories
2. Large type books
I. Title
823.9'14 [F]

ISBN 1–84617–303–5

Published by
F. A. Thorpe (Publishing)
Anstey, Leicestershire

Set by Words & Graphics Ltd.
Anstey, Leicestershire
Printed and bound in Great Britain by
T. J. International Ltd., Padstow, Cornwall

A Shock For Alan

Friday afternoon! On the long walk from the gate where he'd carefully brought his plane to its stand, Alan Ingram smiled to himself.

'Glad to be off, Alan?' his co-pilot asked, and he agreed. For once his hours were in keeping with most folk.

Since switching from passenger aircraft to freight, his working schedule was more sociable. He had the best of both worlds — his ideal job, flying, and more time to spend with his family.

'With any luck, I'll be home around the same time as Dan gets back from school,' he said. Maybe they could go to a football match tomorrow. He hoped Susan would be home, too, from her college course. He could take them both out for a meal tonight.

Susan needed a break. After all those years of bringing up their children while he was flying round the world, his wife deserved some treats.

And the two of them could do with more time together. They'd always been so close — at least, until she began this design course a couple of years ago.

Alan worried that Susan was taking all this a bit too seriously. It wasn't as if she needed to earn money, after all, not with his salary.

Trekking along the corridor towards the freight office, his thoughts switched to their eldest, Clare, now in her fourth year of medicine at Edinburgh University.

He was so proud of Clare — studious and conscientious, she'd make a fine doctor.

Perhaps Clare might even take time off to come home for the weekend. That would be a bonus!

Jessica was a different matter — all he could hope for from her was an e-mail.

Their bouncy, gregarious middle child had swanned off to Australia on her gap year, and had been in Brisbane last they heard.

Alan and Susan had long ago agreed that the kids shouldn't be wrapped in cotton-wool, but they reserved the right to worry while Jessica was so far away.

'There's the boss man,' the co-pilot said. 'He won't need me, will he?'

'Alan!' Brian Cooper hailed him, as the co-pilot slid thankfully away. 'I need just five minutes of your time.

'I know you're just in from Hong Kong, but we have a big decision to make. I could use your advice.

'And, no, it won't wait,' he added.

No point in arguing. Alan followed Brian to the airline office.

'The word we've expected has arrived from Head Office — I need to make some staff redundant,' Brian said bluntly. 'We need to decide who are the best pilots to retain.'

As senior pilot with the airline, Alan had flown with all the rest at some time or other, and he'd evaluated them for annual reports.

'How on earth do you decide for one guy against another?' he demanded.

'It's a good redundancy package they're offering.' Brian mentioned the sum.

'Wouldn't mind that myself!' Alan laughed.

'You're only forty-seven — we don't want to lose you yet!'

'I can't make an instant decision, though, really.' Alan looked at his boss. 'That wouldn't be fair. I'll think it through. Would it be OK if I phoned you in a couple of days or so?'

'Sure. But remember, you won't necessarily be doing any of your colleagues out of a job. Pilots are always in demand.

'Give you a case in point. Remember Quentin Duffy? He left us, bought himself a business aircraft and set up his own charter company. He did very nicely out of that.'

'Did?' Alan looked sharply at him.

'Tells me he's giving up now, looking for a buyer. Got arthritis.'

All the way home along the M8, Alan thought about Brian's comment.

Now that was an interesting prospect. An independent pilot could pick and choose when and where to fly. Alan could think of a few who would enjoy that way of life — he would himself.

Soon he reached Pollokshields, and his own driveway. But Susan's car wasn't back yet.

Heaving a sigh, Alan reached for his flight bag and took out his keys.

★ ★ ★

'Susan, what are you still doing here? You should have been away long ago!'

Neil Drummond, her tutor, had run into her outside the studio.

'I was just finishing some stuff.' Susan hefted the portfolio under her arm. 'My son's gone ten-pin bowling with his mates, and you never know with Alan — flights don't always run to

5

schedule. No fault of the pilot!'

Neil pushed his hands in his pockets. 'Time for a coffee?'

Was that loneliness in his tone? Susan had been told Neil had really never got over the loss of his wife three years ago . . . How awful to be going home to an empty house! Surely she could spare half an hour?

'Why not?' She smiled at him, and he relieved her of the portfolio.

A Listening Ear

'More good things in here for Monday?'

'Hope so. If they are any good, it's your doing. You're so good about listening — helping me to fix my ideas.

'I'm still kind of wary of talking things over with the others — they might think me a bit of a fuddy-duddy!'

'Nonsense,' he scoffed.

But it wasn't. In fact, Neil was the *only* person who really listened to her. She'd tried so hard to get Alan interested in what the course was doing for her, forcing her to use her brain and develop ideas.

Alan was the one she wanted to share it all with, and yet . . .

Oh, he was polite enough when she mentioned her course, but as soon as she got enthusiastic about something, she could see his mind drifting away. And that small core of disappointment inside her wouldn't go away.

For the first time in their married life, there was something important to her that they weren't sharing.

As for the rest of the family, Dan, of course, just let her get on with it. Like most fourteen-year-olds, he knew his mother was on a different planet.

Jessica, though, was their 'go for it' girl. Susan really missed her younger daughter's zest for life and happy encouragement.

And Australia was so far away!

Clare had been supportive up till now, too, but their last phone chat, a few days ago, had been a bit puzzling.

'I've got all these marvellous ideas just queuing up in my imagination, bursting to get out!' Susan had said.

'Good for you, Mum.' Clare's voice had been flat.

'Trust me to be an arty bore, darling!' Susan laughed. 'Your course must be so much more exciting and fulfilling.'

There was silence for so long that Susan thought they'd been cut off.

'I suppose it looks that way,' Clare said at last. 'Noble and admirable, and all that.'

'But it's hard work, too, I realise.' Susan was puzzled by Clare's choice of words.

'Got to go — lecture time. Take care.'

This time Clare had switched off her phone before Susan even had the chance to say goodbye.

She just hoped the problem wasn't too serious. Perhaps Clare had fallen out with her boyfriend . . . though Will was the placid type.

As she and Neil descended into the

8

college's basement bar, Susan put the niggling worry about Clare on the back burner. It would be good to unwind with a chat to Neil.

Clare's Confession

'Clare!' It took Marion Bailie all of two seconds to recognise all was not well with her granddaughter.

'What a nice surprise. Come away in, hen.'

It wouldn't do to let her granddaughter know she'd noticed anything.

Clare would tell her what was up in her own good time.

Marion often wished that her eldest grandchild would let rip, just once.

'Home for the weekend?' she asked, as Clare followed her into the kitchen.

'No!' Clare's answer was so out of character that Marion froze in the act of filling the kettle.

'Sorry, Gran,' Clare went on. 'I don't want Mum and Dad to know I'm in

Glasgow. I can't face them yet.'

'Oh, dear, and I've run out of chocolate biscuits,' Marion murmured, to be rewarded, as she'd hoped, with a faint giggle.

Whatever ailed Clare in all her twenty-two years, her gran had always had a chocolate biscuit to hand to comfort her. The old joke never failed to bring them closer.

Marion made the tea, and turned to find Clare slumped on a chair, her head resting on folded hands on the table.

She felt a lurch of dread. This was no chocolate biscuit problem.

'Right, let's take things into the living-room — much more comfortable.' Marion loaded the tray.

'Carry it through for me, please — I have to phone one of my French group.'

Clare nodded.

Marion had retired from teaching French several years ago, but still held a small weekly class in her flat for folk who wanted to brush up their skills.

She did have to contact one of the

group, but kept the call brief.

She wouldn't be able to make the concert that evening, she apologised.

'It's family,' was her brief excuse and Lizzie understood. Being a mother and grandmother always came first with Marion.

Clare was gazing listlessly out of the window at Bellahouston Park, without seeing a thing.

Marion pushed a cup towards her granddaughter and edged a plate of scones nearer.

Marion wouldn't force Clare to eat or speak — it had always been the way between them, and it had always worked.

'I've made a huge mistake, Gran,' Clare said eventually, crumbling a scone between her fingers.

'What kind?' Marion forced herself to speak naturally.

'I've deceived people. They think I'm a better person than I really am.' Clare was still looking blankly out of the window.

Marion let a few seconds go by.

'You think you've let someone down?'

'Everyone!' At last Clare looked at her.

'That's pretty sweeping,' Marion said mildly.

'And Will wants us to go to Africa,' Clare added.

So the boyfriend *was* involved — yet the two statements didn't seem to have any connection.

'I'm no use to anyone! And you're the only one who'll understand.'

But would she? If this problem was as desperate and complex as it sounded, Marion feared that, for the first time in her granddaughter's life, she might be out of her depth.

Marion had formed a natural bond with Clare when she was tiny, but fundamental problems like these were different. Marion knew she'd feel disloyal to Susan — and Alan — if she cut them out here.

She knew only too well, heartbreakingly, in fact, the devastating effects of advice from the wrong person.

'Your dad's home this weekend, isn't he?' she said tentatively. 'I'm sure he and Mum would want to help. Would you like to give them a ring?'

'Gran, I can't. I couldn't face them.' Clare's voice was tight with tension.

'The thing is, I don't think I can go back to Edinburgh. I can't finish my course, and how can I possibly tell them that?'

'You're Late'

Barely a mile away, Susan swung her car on to the gravel drive. It always gave her such a sense of comfort to be home. The sturdy, century-old stone house appealed to the traditionalist in her — and held the folk she loved best.

It wasn't a typical Pollokshields mansion; Susan reckoned the builder hadn't enough space on the corner site to provide another ten-roomer.

'I'm starved!' Dan announced from the passenger seat, pushing open the car door, and Susan released the boot switch.

'Don't forget your gear!'

He turned on his heel and dragged his school bag, sports bag and sundry other items essential to his well-being from the boot. The shopping bags were somehow overlooked.

As she got out of the car, Susan saw Alan's, parked neatly round the side of the house. He must have arrived on time for once.

She should have been home for him, one voice cried inside her, while another pointed out if she'd come straight home, she'd have missed that vital conversation with Neil.

She hoped Alan would want to hear about her project for next year. She'd have to start it over the summer, of course . . .

If only she could guarantee this weekend would be harmonious! Somehow, an edginess had crept into their relationship, and Susan was sure Alan couldn't enjoy it any more than she did.

She reached the door just as Daniel's bags hit the hall floor.

'Hi, Dad.' Daniel streaked past Alan

and made for the kitchen.

A pity he couldn't see the disappointment in Alan's face at the casual greeting, Susan thought.

'You're late,' Alan said, and they exchanged a brief kiss.

'Daniel went bowling after school. It seemed sensible to stay on at college and pick him up on the way home.'

'If you'd phoned to check, I could have picked him up.'

'I thought you might have had a long enough day, flying in from the Far East.'

They were at it again, Susan realised, dancing round the real problem — not working as a unit any longer.

Or maybe she was just being over-sensitive. Alan had every right to be tired after his journey.

'What's for dinner?' Daniel yelled from the kitchen.

'I thought we might go out,' Alan said quickly.

'Good! Burgers and Coke.' Daniel came through and headed for the stairs. 'I'll get into my jeans.'

'Bags, boots and clobber,' Susan reminded him.

'Don't forget, Mum, I'll need all my stuff washed ready for tomorrow!' He gave her a beatific grin.

'Tomorrow?'

'Yep. Chas's dad says we can set off after lunch, so you have the whole morning to wash and press your son and heir's coolest gear.'

'Set off for where?' Alan said sharply.

Susan carried the shopping into the kitchen, and he followed her.

'Chas's parents are taking him and Daniel to their caravan at Loch Sween for a few days. Until Tuesday.'

'Don't they have school next week?'

'Teacher in-service days. The boys don't go back until Wednesday.'

To The Island

'For heaven's sake!' Alan sat down and stared at her. 'I was hoping to spend some time with my son, since I have the week off. We could all have gone away over the weekend.'

'It was arranged at the last minute, and anyway, he'll be back on Tuesday evening.' She smiled.

'And back at school on Wednesday! And presumably you'll be at college all next week?'

Susan unpacked the groceries with slow deliberation.

'It's term time for me, too, Alan, and I have to start work on a new project this weekend if I'm to get decent results on my course work.'

She glanced at her husband. His mouth was a tight line.

'I'm sorry, Alan. I'd like everything to fit into your schedule, but there are other things going on in our lives.'

The blunt words were out before she could stop them, but Alan only shrugged.

'Of course. Luckily, it's time I went over to the island to see my mother and Gavin. I'll phone her now, see if it's suitable.'

He went out, muttering, but just loud

enough for Susan to hear.

'That is, if *they* have space in their lives for me.'

'That's not fair,' she called after him. 'Dan's at the age when friends matter much more than his crumbly old parents!'

She heard the extension being lifted in the living-room, and sighed impatiently.

Alan had missed much of this stage where the girls were concerned. Susan had weathered it single-handed, and it hadn't occurred to her to mention it to Alan at the time. She did try to cushion him from trivial worries at home.

The family meal out could not be said to be an unqualified success. Alan insisted on going somewhere 'posh and boring', in Daniel's words, which were almost the only ones he uttered all evening.

Susan was used to his mood, but Alan was annoyed, and she was glad when they got home.

'I'd better get started on Daniel's washing,' she said. 'Anything you need in a hurry?'

'No, thanks,' Alan said. 'I'll be taking casual stuff to the island.'

'You're going to see your mother, then?' He hadn't said a word about that over dinner.

'I'll leave tomorrow, get out from under your feet.' His tone was cold. 'There'll be room for me at Fearchar.'

'Alan, it's not like that . . . ' she began, but he went on, unheeding.

'I'm not sure how long I'll stay. I'll ring to let you know when I'm coming back.'

And he switched on the TV.

Susan stood, frozen, by the washing machine, Daniel's shirts and socks still in a bundle in her hands.

When Alan had said he was leaving tomorrow, she'd felt relieved! Whatever was happening to them?

A Gulf Between Them

As the ferry left Oban on a fine May morning, Alan felt better. There was

19

nowhere in the world to touch the west of Scotland for clarity of blue sky, purity of air, and the lively freshness of the sea.

The ferry skirted Mull, and its mountains dominated the grandeur of the view.

You could keep most of the rest of the world, Alan thought. Scotland was magical.

He could already make out the island of Bradan, where the ferry was bound. Still out of sight was Heronsay, his birthplace, separated from Bradan by a narrow, dangerous strait.

It was such a change of gear for him, to be standing on a boat letting someone else worry about the driving. Almost like being a lad again.

Ever since he'd been a small boy, Alan's fascination with aircraft of all descriptions hadn't lessened. He was lucky to be among the few who were paid for doing something they loved.

He watched the gulls winging over the waves, and smiled. He'd passed on that fascination and passion to his children. Both Clare and Jessica already had their private pilot's licences, and Daniel could hardly wait till he was old enough to sit the exam.

Daniel. Bother the boy.

If only Alan hadn't growled so much at him on Friday evening! He'd try to make it up to him when he got back home.

And then there was Susan. This blasted course was creating a gulf between them, and she couldn't, or wouldn't, see it.

Well, before he left on his next flight on Saturday, he'd have to do something about that.

The last stages of the journey unwound themselves, and Alan unwound with them. It was just like coming home from school, except that he took a taxi along to Fiadh, on the tip of Bradan — the bus ran only on school days.

'Ruairidh! Great to see you.' Alan shook the man's hand and hopped into the Fearchar launch.

'Aye, Alan, long time.'

'Glad you could meet me.'

'Aye, well, I managed to deliver the post before I came for you, this being my second journey, you understand. I'll finish mowing the lawns before I go to the shop — some problem with the plumbing, I'm to understand.'

Ruairidh started the engine, and Alan hid a smile.

If anything needed mended, cultivated or built on Heronsay, Ruairidh was on hand to do it. He seemed to know how by instinct, and experience garnered over the years he'd lived on the island, the precise number of which no-one was permitted to know.

'Calm today.' Alan nodded at the strait.

'Deceiving.' A short silence fell.

Gavin Lamont had been Alan's best friend all his life. He'd been Laird of Heronsay since the evening twenty-two years ago when Gavin's father had insisted on taking the old boat across without Ruairidh at the wheel.

The boat had foundered on treacherous rocks during a sudden squall, and both Gavin's parents had been lost.

'Mum said there were no visitors at Fearchar at the moment?' Alan said.

'There's a party arriving next week, six, I think — that'll mean two journeys. One to ferry the folk over, then the second the fetch the luggage.

'I'll never understand how folk need more than one pair of breeks, shoes and whatever for a few days' stay on a small island.' Ruairidh's tone was just short of scathing.

Gavin's house, Fearchar, was just coming into sight, set on a slight rise above the Heronsay jetty. On either side of the central tower were double-fronted wings. The early sun was reflected in the long windows, softening the effect of the ancient walls.

The original Fearchar had been one of the first Lamonts. Gavin had always said he'd name his first son after him.

Opposite Fearchar, in the lee of the hill, stood the Ingram family croft. Alan and Gavin had grown up together, attended schools on Bradan together and forged a lasting and close friendship.

A Warm Welcome

Within minutes, Alan was on his way to the open front door of Fearchar.

The dogs were after him at once, of course, and he was given an ecstatic welcome.

'Down, idiots.' He fended the black Labradors off, laughing. 'Hello, Grouse — hello, Heather.'

'Alan!'

All three of them turned as the laird came downstairs.

Gavin Lamont was one of the few men Alan knew who could look right in the kilt on every occasion. He came bounding down the grand staircase of Fearchar, kilt swinging, leather jerkin open over a checked shirt, brogues on his feet, and socks that didn't match.

They took up the conversation where they'd last left it a few months ago, and then another voice broke in indignantly while the dogs fawned round them.

'Would you look at that! And he has the matched socks in his drawer, too!'

'Mum!'

Before he gave her a hug, Alan gazed at Eileen.

Yes, she looked great for sixty-seven, clearly still loving her job as Gavin's housekeeper. She'd moved back to the island when they'd lost Dad ten years earlier.

'So how's the new venture?' Alan asked, kissing his mother.

Gavin had just opened Fearchar as a rather grand guesthouse, to help offset the cost of keeping up the estate.

'Fine. Get away now, Grouse, excitement over!' Gavin patted the dog, and led the way down the hall. 'Fine, mostly thanks to your mum, of course.'

'Get away with you,' Eileen said briskly. 'The girls do it all. It's wonderful what a Heronsay lass can accomplish in a four-hour shift — the part-time roles were all Gavin's idea.'

She winked at the laird, who grinned at Alan.

'I wonder who put that idea into my head?' he asked innocently, as they went into the kitchen, which smelled of fresh scones.

'Family fine?' Eileen asked, making coffee.

'Absolutely.'

'How's Susan enjoying her course?' Gavin asked. 'I have so much admiration for her, taking that on. Mind you, she's always had a good eye for colour and design.'

Alan was silent. That was a bit of a jolt. Why did it take Gavin to notice a talent in Susan that he hadn't?

'She's ploughed a hard row, bringing up the children with you away all the time,' his mother commented. 'I expect she's getting a lot of fun out of being a student again. Brings her closer to the kids, too, in a way.'

Alan felt nothing less than shocked.

He'd never seen this course of Susan's as more than a whim to fill empty days. He sipped his coffee and spread butter on a scone, silent.

If Mum and Gavin were taking Susan seriously, what had he been missing?

'Coffee, Ruairidh?' Eileen called from the back door.

'No time!'

'He doesn't change.' Alan grinned.

'Not quite true.' Gavin frowned. 'He'd never admit it, but Ruairidh's slowing down. And I'm beginning to worry about our guests coming across in the power boat, after the tedious journey from Oban and beyond.'

Alan shrugged.

'What's the alternative?' Then Alan noticed that Gavin was grinning as if he'd lost a penny and found a pound.

'He won't rest till you've seen his latest big idea,' Eileen said with resignation. 'You'd better get it over with.'

Alan raised his eyebrows, but his mother gave nothing away, so he followed Gavin out to the hall again.

'It's good to be back,' he said, allowing the atmosphere of Fearchar to enfold him.

Mellow wood panelled the walls, matching the great staircase. The upper gallery was hung with portraits like the ones in similar great family homes all over Scotland — ancestors in stiff poses, but impressive, for all that.

He glanced down at the familiar mosaic design on the hall floor. Susan had always raved about it, he remembered. Was that an example of her good eye?

'You're going to think I'm mad,' Gavin said, going out of the front door, 'but I just had to have it.'

Still mystified, Alan followed him, round the side of Fearchar, past the huge conservatory he always thought of as a cousin of the Kibble Palace in Glasgow. The grapes and peaches which grew there, under Ruairidh's careful management, wouldn't be ripe for a while yet.

Next they passed the doveocote, and some of the birds fluttered up. Glancing up, Alan remembered that Gavin had christened two of the doves Alan and Susan on their wedding day here on Heronsay, over twenty-three years ago.

There hadn't been a lot of billing and cooing lately, and whose fault was it?

'Are you taking me to the football pitch?' Alan was puzzled.

Beyond a small stand of trees there was the rough field which served as football pitch for every boy on the island.

Gavin cleared the trees and pointed.

'Now, tell me what you think of that!' He beamed, and Alan's jaw dropped.

Jessica Is Worried

The sun was shining in Brisbane, too, that day. Jessica Ingram sat on the deck of the Petersons' house, sipping a mango smoothie and lazily watching the CityCat ferries zig-zagging across the water, carrying people from homes to schools, shops and offices.

The house was in the elegant suburb of Hamilton, built on hills which overlooked the snaking river.

This wasn't what a gap year was supposed to be like, Jessica reflected happily. It was all too comfortable and cosy, and not at all adventurous.

'Are you still in touch with our Year Seven crowd?' Dawn Peterson asked, and Jessica screwed up her eyes to think back to primary school, when the Petersons had still lived in Glasgow.

'I lost track of some folk when I went to the Academy,' she admitted.

'I was half in love with that McLean boy.' Dawn giggled.

'When you were eleven?' Jessica laughed.

'Oh, well, you know me, the romantic type.'

'Presumably emigrating to Australia has made it worse,' Jessica teased. 'All these handsome bronzed blokes, into rugby and surfing.'

'No, I'm true to Ricky now.' Dawn smiled at her. 'I'm a one-man girl. What about you?'

Jessica drained the last of her smoothie. Dawn's boyfriend was OK, but she felt that her old friend still had a lot of living to do.

'I plan to fall in love time and again. Maybe half a dozen times while I'm here.' She stretched out on the lounger, grinning at the expression on Dawn's face.

'You'll see plenty of men in that bar you're insisting on working in,' Dawn said, a trifle primly.

Jessica said nothing.

The Petersons might not approve of her part-time job in the bar on Racecourse Road, but bar work was easy to get for a backpacker. Actually, she loved the buzz, the laughter, the joshing.

But it was only temporary. She was determined to move around and see the country. That was what a gap year was all about!

Her parents had only agreed to her coming halfway round the world on her own if she stayed with the Petersons, their old neighbours from Glasgow.

Jessica had only been in the place a week before she realised she had to find a way to detach herself.

'Oh, gosh, I haven't checked my e-mails today!' She ran into the bedroom to fetch the laptop Dad had insisted on buying for her.

There was a message from Clare. Jessica could see her sister now, sitting at the computer in her flat.

Clare was so like their mother, in her neat physique and dark colouring. Jessica herself was all Ingram, with her height and uncontrollable fair hair.

Maybe I should get it cut short, she thought, like Dad's, or even worse, Daniel's.

No, that was carrying things too far!

Clare's message seemed to be mainly about deciding to go back to Edinburgh after a brief visit to Gran.

Jessica read it again. What wasn't she

getting here? Why did Clare go to Gran's, not home? No news of the parents or Daniel.

And where else would she go apart from Edinburgh?

E-mails were fine, but there was nothing to beat speaking to someone. The tone of voice could tell you a lot.

It was time she set off for the bar, though, and anyway entirely the wrong time of day to call Britain.

The races were over for the day at Doomben, and the bar was crowded.

'Jez!' The cry of greeting went up as she appeared behind the counter. She'd had the job for a bare hour before her name had been abbreviated, in the way Australians have. She loved it!

The bar was crowded, and she was kept busy.

As she delivered an order to a table in the corner, she noticed Steve Berry was one of the group, and her heart gave a tiny flip.

She'd noticed him on her very first

day in the bar — tall, rangy and very attractive.

Maybe this is the first of my six experiences of falling in love, she thought.

It didn't matter much, anyway, Steve had barely noticed her on the other race days. He didn't spend much time in the bar.

Being a vet, he was busy on duty with the horses most of the day; then he disappeared off into the country, where he looked after horses on stud farms.

'Jez, I'd love your autograph on this.' One of the group, Vic, displayed his right arm, encased in a plaster cast.

'Oh. no. How'd you do that?' She signed *Jez* with a flourish. 'We call this a stookie in Scotland.'

The group roared with laughter.

'Stookie the pilot. Good on yer. Vic.'

'You're not a pilot, not with a broken arm?' Jez looked at Vic with sympathy.

'My pilot, too,' Steve remarked. 'His plane's sitting out there waiting to take me back home, with no-one to fly it.

And I have horses waiting for me.'

Jez put the empty tray on the table.

'I have a pilot's licence,' she said.

Alan's Plans

When the ferry docked at Oban, Alan could hardly wait to reach his car. He headed for Crianlarich, the first stop on the way to the airport. Brian Potter had said he'd had time to see him.

Alan remembered the thrill of elation he'd felt when he saw the Sikorsky standing on the football field. Gavin had bought a helicopter!

'What do you think, Alan? My guests are coming over for a spot of spoiling, a bit of R & R, and that journey takes for ever. We've been losing bookings because of it.'

'Whatever happened to the proposed causeway between Bradan and Heronsay? You've been after that for ages.'

'Bradan Council won't meet the shared costs. So when I heard about this little bird being for sale, I just had to have it.'

Alan inspected every inch of the machine, and was as elated as the laird.

'The only thing is, I need someone to fly it for me. How do I get hold of a pilot?'

Alan's hands were on the controls by now. He didn't blurt anything out, but his mind was working furiously. Thank heavens he'd kept up his chopper licence.

All the pieces of the jigsaw — like being with his family, forging a proper relationship with Daniel, being closer to Susan yet still doing a job he loved — fell neatly into place.

'You've got one,' he said calmly.

'You? Alan, that would be perfect! But I seem to remember you have a job?'

Alan explained about the redundancy package on offer.

'I've thought a lot about it, and maybe now's the time for me to go it alone — set myself up in business.'

Their Good Idea

Sitting in Gavin's study, they talked it through. If Alan had his own charter company, Gavin could hire him as pilot when needed.

'The guests won't even need to travel further than any Scottish airport. If I get my hands on an Islander, say, and you have the chopper, we can fly them from most places to Heronsay,' Alan pointed out.

'Mm. We could advertise much more widely in that case — and the website might begin to pay for itself.'

'We could really make this whole thing pay, Gavin.' Alan leaned forward. 'We could act as a ferry for Heronsay folk. A school contract?'

Eileen had been sitting in on the discussions.

'You could get a grant for that — Bradan Council wouldn't need to run buses to and from Diadh any longer.' She paused.

'Alan, where are you going to be

based — Glasgow?'

'No, I need to be here. If it's OK with you, Mum, we could take over the croft?'

His mother's face lit up.

'Have you and Susan and the family here? Oh, Alan, that would be just fine!'

'Where's the plane going to land?' Gavin asked. 'We'll need more than a helipad.'

'What's wrong with the beach at Cladch?'

On the far side of the island was a mile-long stretch of silver sand, rarely affected by tides.

'Just like the one at Barra!' Eileen cried.

'Alan, we have to do this.' Gavin stretched, and smiled. 'We'll be able to attract more guests with such good transport, but still keep the island unspoiled — as it has to be.'

Alan's first stumbling-block was his boss. Brian Potter was most reluctant to accept his request for redundancy.

'This wasn't what I had in mind at

all! But one look at your face tells me I'm not going to change your mind. And yes, OK, I'll give you Quentin's phone number.'

Alan left the airport still buzzing with excitement. He'd managed to talk the boss round.

Brian had agreed to Alan making one more freight flight, then taking redunancy.

That would give the family the whole summer to settle in on the island. Even considering the cost of the plane, they'd be very well off. The redundancy package, plus the money they'd have from the sale of the Glasgow house, would see to that. There would be business start-up grants, too.

The family would be together, and he'd have achieved his dream — his own charter company!

Alan had always planned to train as a flying instructor. His first pupil would be Daniel!

Susan Hears The News

Head reeling with excitement, he arrived home just after Susan, who was in the living-room. He went straight to her, taking her in his arms and whirling her round. He landed a kiss on her nose.

'I have got the most fantastic news!' He sat beside her on the sofa. Holding her hand in his, he told her everything.

His enthusiasm carried him away. All his plans, all his dreams, spilled out, and at first he didn't notice how quiet she was.

Then she took her hand away, and he looked at her properly. Her face was white.

'Let me get this straight, Alan. You've done all this — redundancy, setting up in partnership with Gavin — without even mentioning it to me?' Her voice was shaking.

'Time was of the essence, love — Gavin needs to set this up for his summer visitors. And I had to see Brian right away before he made someone else redundant and, well, it all just took off! Sorry about the pun.' He laughed, still euphoric.

'Well, it isn't taking off for me, Alan.' Her tone was icy, and he stared at her.

'I don't want any part of this, and if you'd any sense at all, you'd have realised it!'

A Dream Come True

'How could you do this to us?' Susan's voice was unsteady as she stared at Alan. 'Do what? It's brilliant! What's wrong? It's a whole new way of life for us all!'

'*You* think that.' Susan felt her temper rising. 'Personally, I don't feel there's anything wrong with life as it is. There's no need to turn it upside down!'

'Really?' Alan's reply was loaded with meaning.

'All right, maybe it hasn't been ideal

with you away so much, but that was the career you chose — and loved. And I went along with it.'

'Susan, hasn't it ever occurred to you that I might have grown tired of being just an employee? That if I'm going to make a dream come true, I'd better start now?'

'Yes, of course it's crossed my mind! But this is the first time you've mentioned it, and that's the problem here.'

'What do you mean by that?'

'For heaven's sake, Alan, how can you spring something as momentous as this right out of the blue?

'Not even a phone call from Heronsay! You've talked this over with Gavin, but you haven't given a thought to discussing with me the huge problems this will raise for the family.'

'So it's quite different from you going off and signing up for a three-year design course without thinking what effect it would have on the family?'

Susan sat down suddenly, sick at

heart. What was going on in Alan's mind?

She took time to think before she spoke.

'Clearly you don't remember, but I took a whole year to decide about the course. During that time we talked it over, all five of us. Correct me if I'm wrong, but I seem to remember that you encouraged me.'

'Of course I agreed! How could I deny you something you said you really wanted? What you can't see is that it's taken over all our lives.'

That was simply unfair, but she knew Alan — he'd never see it in those terms, any more than he could see this new venture would totally disrupt their lives.

It was Alan all over — charging off after new ideas like a bull at a gate without thinking of the consequences.

The silence was lengthening now, and Susan thought how much she hated it.

Up till now, they'd been the sort of close-knit family where everything was aired. They'd promised each other that at the very start of their marriage.

As if reading her mind, Alan suddenly joined her on the sofa.

'I just want us all to be together, Susan. This seems an ideal way, as well as being a profitable business. I know it would mean you giving up this particular course, but there are distance learning ones, aren't there? You'd easily qualify for one of those.'

'I could have done a distance course years ago. It's being with the other students — having the teachers challenge you . . . ' She tailed off. Alan would never understand.

'I know you'll be hankering after Glasgow, but we'll be just a short helicopter jump away.' He laughed. 'Gavin can't believe things are working out so well.'

Gavin again! Susan was very fond of Alan's best friend, but right this minute she could have seen him far enough.

'Alan, this isn't about me or my

course, it's about all the family. Have you thought how all this will affect Daniel?'

'Of course I have! Bradan High has an excellent record, as you well know — it's my old school. And you know Dan enjoys the outdoor life — he's never been a city lad.

'As for the girls, Jessica has itchy feet, and Clare's career could take her anywhere in the world. From now on they will be using 'home' as a stopping-off place.'

Susan felt as if she were in shock, but she couldn't give up yet. If she wasn't honest with Alan, where would that leave their marriage?

'Look, Alan, I can see what a marvellous chance this is for you and the business, but I don't want to go and live on Heronsay,' she said quietly.

'Fine.' Alan was on his feet again. 'Break up the family!'

Susan sighed.

'Don't be so pig-headed. This is our home, the one the kids have always known. You can't just whip it away from under them!'

At that moment, the front door crashed open and shut, and Daniel's bag hit the hall floor.

How would Alan handle this?

Daniel's Joy

Daniel catapulted into the living-room.

'So how was the weekend?' Alan asked.

'Magic. So cool! We spent the whole time outside, fishing, hill-walking — we hired mountain bikes, stalked some deer — just for fun, of course.'

'I knew you were a real outdoor type.' Alan took the anorak and boots Daniel shed, and pressed home his advantage. 'How would you like to live on Heronsay?'

'You mean — where Granny Ingram lives? In her cottage where we used to go for holidays? Oh, yeah, cool! Can I ask Chas to come, too?'

'Sure, he can come on holiday. And guess what? Uncle Gavin's bought a helicopter.'

'Who's going to fly it?'

Alan just smiled at his son, and Daniel whooped with joy.

In her heart, Susan knew her husband wasn't trying to manipulate Daniel; he wasn't that kind of person. Enthusiasm for his new project had overcome him, that was all.

Some Ingram gene caused them all to be mad about being airborne. Susan preferred to be on terra firma, but she would never have tried to stop any of the family indulging their passion for flying.

'Mountains of washing in the bag as usual?' Susan hugged Dan on her way past. 'I'll get started.'

As she was leaving the room, she heard Alan's voice.

'My flight doesn't leave until Saturday evening, and I have to go and see a man about a plane. Like to come with me?'

★　★　★

Jessica couldn't believe how good it felt to leave the Petersons' home-from-home in Brisbane, even for a couple of days or so.

'The air charter company is going to need a temporary pilot,' she told them. 'Mum and Dad think I should take the chance. And guess what? Dad's going into the air charter business at home!'

She had one more stint at the bar before going south with Steve to the charter company's airfield. But, this time, she'd be sitting in a passenger seat, not at the controls.

'No offence, but my sister is nineteen and she's still at school,' Steve had drawled.

Vic, his usual pilot, had a chat with her at the bar.

'My colleague, Doug, will be taking the plane and Steve back home. Hitch a ride with him.

'Doug will introduce you to the charter company — it's a small operation, mainly flying guests for the hotel, or stud and stable owners, and vets like Steve.

'I'm sure they'll be looking for a spare pilot, while I'm out of action.'

When they took off from Brisbane Airport, Steve was sitting beside her. He'd been really friendly, giving her advice on what to wear for safety.

'It's open country — it's the wild, the hinterland. Acres of fertile land, fed with streams from the surrounding mountains.

'Years ago it was a drover's route — the Ramrookum Run. It has a new name now — the Land of the Copperhead Snake.' He grinned at her.

'That's why you need stout boots. Remember always to be equipped for the climate when you're out of doors. You can't play games with it.'

'Thanks.' She was touched that this attractive man was taking such an interest in her.

'I'm going to be flying, though — that's not too close to the wildlife!'

He simply smiled, and Jessica seethed.

She would prove to Steve that, nineteen or not, she was a first-class pilot. One day she'd fly him to and from the races!

Perhaps that would help their relationship along . . .

As the plane descended towards the tiny airstrip, Jessica was awestruck. She'd had no conception of how vast this place was.

Acres and acres of pasture stretched away and there were cattle and horses and sheep everywhere. Green fields were surrounded to the south and west by a semi-circle of mountains, purple topped in the warm haze of the late afternoon.

She was reminded of the mountains of Scotland, and felt her first pang of homesickness.

As they came in to land, she could pick out stabling here and there, the hotel Vic had mentioned, and some holiday chalets.

Jessica In The Bush

As the pilot brought the plane to a gentle stop, Jessica saw a pretty young girl waving at them. They jumped down from the plane, and she ran towards them.

'Steve, am I glad to see you! We thought you'd be back yesterday!'

As Steve explained about the delay, Jessica studied the girl. She was maybe fifteen, tall and slim, with long brown hair tied back in a pony tail, but it was her lively face that was so appealing.

'Hi, there,' she greeted Jessica. 'Sorry to make a beeline for Steve, but one of our horses is sick and we need him desperately.'

'This is Kirralee from the trail riding centre,' Steve said.

'I'm Jez. Sorry about your horse,' Jessica murmured sympathetically.

'Good luck.' Steve picked up his bag. 'See you around, I expect.'

Then he and Kirralee walked over to a utility vehicle — it must be his; he'd taken keys from his pocket. Kirralee's horse was hitched to a railing beneath some trees, in the shade. The ute pulled out and the horse followed.

Steve was back on his own territory with a job to do. She had no call on him.

In the airfield office, Doug introduced Jessica to Emery, the manager. He looked over her pilot's licence and papers, then handed them back.

'Nothing for you at the moment, I'm afraid, Jez. One of the planes is being serviced, and Doug's flying someone to Sydney tomorrow. We might need a replacement for Vic in a week or so.'

Jessica thanked them, and walked out into the dusk.

Doug had suggested she might find a room at the hotel for the night, at least. Tomorrow she'd have to arrange a lift to Beaudesert, the nearest town, a half hour's drive away, to find transport back to Brisbane.

She hefted her backpack and made her way towards the hotel, suddenly feeling dwarfed by the vast, empty country around her.

The silence was broken now by hundreds of cicadas, working up to full shriek, and somehow the eerie noise emphasised her loneliness.

'Well, Jez Ingram, this is what you wanted. No more security blankets — you're on your own now!'

She squared her shoulders and climbed the wooden steps to the veranda of the hotel.

The First Guests

Waiting for Alan's inaugural flight to Fearchar, Eileen shaded her eyes. Yes, there was a helicopter, over to the east.

She'd never expected things to move so fast. Ingram Air now consisted of Alan and Gavin as directors, with shares all held by the family. He'd bought that small passenger craft from his old colleague, and was also Gavin's chief pilot.

'Chief pilot?' Gavin had laughingly questioned as they sorted out the legal stuff. 'How many will there be?'

'Only me for a start, but Clare and Jessica might help out when they're around. Then, of course, Daniel, in time.' Alan looked proud.

'That's providing Jessica gets back safely from the land of the copperhead!' Eileen put in, but her son just laughed at her.

'Jessica can take care of herself.'

Eileen had felt a thrill when Jessica's phone call had come through.

'Guess where I am, Granny Eye,' her irrepressible granddaughter had said.

When she had first begun to talk she had named Eileen Granny Eye and Susan's mother Granny Em. The names had stuck.

'In the land of the copperhead snake.'

'Snakes!' Eileen gasped.

'Haven't seen one yet, but I live in hope,' Jessica teased. 'Anyway, I'll be in the air most of the time, I hope.'

'Where's he off to now?' Ruairidh

grumped at her side, as Alan banked to the west.

'Giving them a tour of the island, I expect,' Eileen said bracingly. 'It's a nice idea — none of the guests have been here before.'

'Island folk will not like the noise, believe me. Upsetting all the beasts . . .'

'Once or twice a week?' Eileen said sharply. 'I don't think anyone will object but you, Ruairidh. If this means more folk can get here, with more money to spend, that can only help everyone on Heronsay.'

'I've lost one job already,' Ruairidh grumbled on. 'There's no need for a ferryman now.'

'What rubbish! We're not all going to be flying around. Besides, you've just taken on another job, guiding the helicopter in.'

'That's true, no-one else could do it.' Despite himself, Ruairidh couldn't keep the smugness from his voice.

The helicopter was out of sight now, over Rionnay, where the fishing families lived. Lobster and prawns were their main catches, and Fearchar had the first choice.

Sabhal was the next hamlet, produce from which also supplied Fearchar and Bradan.

The families over there did make a living, but if times were bad, Gavin always stepped in to help. He took his ownership of Heronsay responsibly and as a result, it was a happy place.

Alan would take the helicopter round the bulk of Ben Fuar, with its good hill-walking route, Eileen knew, and then sweep over Loch Fuar, where guests were welcome to fish.

'Here they are, Ruairidh. Time for you to go do your stuff. I'll just call Gavin.'

The laird had to be by the helipad when Alan landed, ready to greet his guests. Two middle-aged, well-dressed couples were first off the aircraft, and Alan handed out fishing rods, along with their luggage, to Ruairidh.

The fifth guest was a Miss Judith

Paton, and Eileen was curious to see the woman who'd requested a room at the back of Fearchar, instead of the more scenic view of the sea.

'Like a hand?' Gavin moved forward to help someone down.

'Gavin Lamont.' He smiled at her.

'No need — I can manage a few steps.'

Judith Paton was much younger than the usual run of guests and, Eileen thought, in need of a good holiday. She was far too thin, and a rather set expression spoiled what could be a bonnie face.

'I'm Eileen, the housekeeper.' She stepped forward. 'We're quite informal here.'

Miss Paton looked at her, then surprised Eileen with a not unfriendly nod.

'Good, that suits me.'

She turned back to the helicopter to take an artist's easel from Alan, and Gavin led his guests towards the house.

Finally, Alan passed over the last bag

and came to give his mother a hug.

'Trouble.' He nodded after the guests.

'Miss Paton?'

'I think Gavin's going to have his hands full!' He stretched his arms. 'I'm going up to the croft now, Mum. I've measured some of the furniture, to see how it will fit in.'

'You're really all going to move up here?' Eileen was cautious. During the last few weeks, she'd heard absolutely nothing from Susan, which was unlike her.

There had never been any problems between them, and Eileen had great admiration for her daughter-in-law, coping as she did with a growing family and Alan's frequent absences.

But Susan's life had always been centred in Glasgow, and Eileen had grave misgivings about how she must be feeling.

'Of course!' Alan answered her question with a determination that made Eileen feel uneasy. 'IngramAir is

on its way up, Mum, and it belongs
here on Heronsay.'

A Great Chance

While Alan was away setting up his new
business, Susan was back at art college.

For once, she kept close to her fellow
students, accepting lunch invitations.

While she was with them, part of a
laughing, chattering group, she didn't
need to think — or to worry.

She was using them, no doubt of
that, but she could think of no other
way to avoid her tutor.

She was in such a state that Susan
knew one kind word from him would
see her blurting out all her worries.

Neil would be a sympathetic listener,
but Alan was the man who ought to be
listening to her — and he'd simply
refused to hear anything he didn't want
to hear.

There was a cold lump of dread
within her. Every time she tried to

discuss the future with Alan, it ended in fruitless argument.

She didn't grudge him his achievement with his own company for a second — she was very proud of him. Yet the price was too high for her.

Surely they could still stay in their own home in Glasgow and Alan could commute? Heronsay was barely an hour away!

Of course, now that he'd bought Quentin Duffy's plane, his redundancy money had gone. He couldn't afford to run two homes. So why bother with a second one on Heronsay?

Back at college after lunch, she found a message from Neil, who needed to discuss something with her after the lecture.

'Shall we go along to my study?' he asked when all the other students had filed out.

That wasn't a good idea, Susan thought.

'Couldn't we just talk here? I'm dashing off to Edinburgh as soon as possible. My son is having a sleepover, so it's a good opportunity to visit my eldest and catch up on girlie chat.'

It was the only excuse she could think of.

Neil looked disappointed, but he fished in his pocket and brought out a brochure.

'I wanted to show you these details. It's a summer school on interior design, being held down in Somerset during August.'

'Really?' Susan took the brochure from him. 'You think I should apply?'

'I think you should really concentrate on interior design. You have a real talent, Susan, and I see your future career going in that direction.'

Those were almost the most exciting words she'd heard.

'I think the course would be of immense value to you. Will you please think about it?'

'Yes, of course I will.' Susan could hardly get the words out, she was so excited.

'Something to think about while

you're driving to Edinburgh?' he prompted.

Jolted back to reality, she thanked him and left the lecture theatre.

She sat in the car for a few minutes, savouring the fact Neil thought she had a career in front of her. Then she opened the brochure to look at the course structure — and discovered the tutor for the summer school was Neil himself.

Driving along the M8 took all her concentration. She couldn't wait to see Clare. If she didn't discuss Alan's plans with someone, she'd go mad.

This was all about their home. How could Alan turn his back on the house where they'd lived practically all their married life, the only home the children knew? It was the centre of their lives. It was precious!

Eileen would understand her worries, but she could hardly confide in her mother-in-law. She'd be loyal to Alan above all, as any mother would.

As for Marion, her own mother,

Susan knew if she told her it would be a cruel and harsh reminder of a dreadful, unresolved family break-up many years ago.

Her oldest daughter was the one person Susan felt she could discuss this with. Jessica's gap year was shaping up nicely; there was no way Susan could spell out problems at home.

And Daniel didn't think much further ahead than his next football practice. He was so keen to get a place on the team for his year.

But Clare's practical mind would grasp things instantly. Just discussing her problems would help Susan to put things in perspective.

Clare's Confession

She drove straight to Clare's student flat in Warrender Park.

'Mum!' Clare was clearly astonished to see her, and Susan had the shock of her life as she looked at her daughter.

Clare was undoubtedly thinner than when she'd been home last, and her complexion was ashen. It was near exam time, though — she was probably overdoing the studying.

The fragility was even more obvious when they hugged.

'Can I make some coffee?' Susan asked.

'Sure! Forgetting my manners.' Clare managed a shaky smile, and led her mother into the kitchen. 'Ignore the mess.'

Susan did. With four girls sharing the flat, it was difficult to keep tidy all the time.

Clare produced a packet of biscuits and Susan took one — soggy, close to being stale. She wished she'd thought of bringing some food.

'Clare, I came to discuss this problem — ' she began.

'Granny told you!' Clare exploded. 'She said she wouldn't! She promised!'

'I wasn't ready to talk to you about this, Mum — that's why I went specially through to see her. I needed someone to listen, and it wasn't fair on you and Dad.'

Listening to all this, Susan felt as if icy water was replacing her blood in her veins. This was her Clare, her reliable, steady daughter?

She remembered that phone conversation — was it only a couple of weeks ago? — when she'd thought Clare was upset about something. How could she have ignored that warning sign?

'Granny told me nothing.' She fought to keep her voice steady.

'I didn't even know you'd gone to see her.'

Why not come to us? But she knew better than to voice the words.

'I'm here now. But if you're not ready to tell me, then that's OK, too,' she lied.

Clare burst into tears.

'I want to leave university,' she sobbed.

'You must have a strong reason for that, after four years.' Susan tried to sound calm.

'I'm not cut out to be a doctor!' Clare reached for her coffee and took a gulp.

'But it's what you've always wanted,' Susan reminded her gently.

'What I thought I wanted, but I'm the wrong person. Oh, I like all the theory, and some of the practice, but . . . it's the patients.'

'You're getting too involved in their problems?'

'No, I understand all their problems. I know about their illnesses, and the treatments they need, but they're not real to me.

'I don't feel in touch with them as people. They're . . . they're just bodies!'

Susan searched desperately for a response, but this was quite outside her experience. Clare needed expert help to guide her through this.

'I've let you down, all of you!' Clare went on. 'You and Dad believe in me — and when I think of all the money you've invested in me! I'm no use. Not fit for medicine.'

'Clare, the money's not important — you are. What do you want to do?'

'I want to come home. It sounds pathetic, but I need to be there, with you and Dad and Daniel. I just need to have my own place, my room, my things.' Clare dashed tears away from her cheeks.

Susan stayed in Edinburgh that night, in Clare's bed, while her daughter slept on the sofa.

They had talked into the small hours, and it had helped. Without prompting, Clare had decided to finish the term, then come home and think.

'One step at a time,' Susan had said in the end. 'It's the only way.'

Next morning, Susan joined the rush hour on the M8. She'd decided to skip college, go home and get some sleep, and then contact Alan on Heronsay. He had to know about Clare right away.

Turning into the drive, she was surprised to see a man ringing her doorbell. He turned round at the sound of her car. He had a clipboard in his hand, she saw.

'Mrs Ingram? I'm Martin Speirs from the property agency. Your husband asked me to arrange the sale of your house.'

A Family Home

The Ingram croft on Heronsay had been there for generations. Alan's forebear had chosen the land carefully, and built his cottage in a sheltered spot — opposite the rear of Fearchar, which protected it from the sea winds, with its gable end at the foot of the slope leading up to Balderry Hill.

When he walked in that morning, Alan felt a surge of nostalgia. The cottage had been empty since his mother moved to Fearchar as house-keeper, but it was kept aired.

He drifted round, touching a piece of furniture here, taking long-forgotten books from shelves there. It was a real family home — just begging to be occupied again . . .

'Alan!' He heard his mother calling as she approached the cottage.

'Susan's been on the phone.' She joined him in the living-room. 'She wants you to call her back as soon as possible.'

Alan nodded. Maybe he'd take his time over that.

Presumably she'd met the estate agent. He'd tried to warn her about the visit, but she hadn't been home.

'What do you think of a sun-room?' he asked. 'There's nothing outside the gable end facing the hill — we've never cultivated anything there. It would be an ideal place to build on.'

'Him.' His mother looked at him. 'Aye, well, space is going to be a priority, Alan. There's a big difference between the five of you coming here for a couple of weeks in the summer, and settling in to live. And a grown-up family, at that.'

'It will be just Susan, Daniel and me. The girls will probably only come on short visits.' He wandered into the kitchen.

'What about all your furniture from Glasgow — where will that go?' his mother persisted.

'There'll be plenty of room once we've extended the place,' Alan said airily.

'Oh, aye. Ten rooms you have at the moment, isn't it?

'Since there's only three bedrooms upstairs, where will you and Susan work?' She followed Alan into the kitchen and began absent-mindedly buffing up the pristine stainless steel sink.

'Work?' He looked puzzled.

'Well, I know you've been using a room at Fearchar as the Ingram Air office, but I thought that was only temporary. And then there's Susan's work to be considered.'

'Mm.' Alan wasn't prepared to be drawn into a discussion.

'I think you should phone Susan now,' Eileen said firmly. 'And get the phone put on again down here. I'm not trekking all the way down every time you have a message.'

'I left my mobile at the big house — I'll follow you down, Mum.'

At least the walk would give him time to brace himself for the inevitable argument.

But it didn't come.

'Alan, it's Clare,' Susan told him as soon as she heard his voice. 'She's in a bit of a state. She wants to leave university.'

'What? Why on earth — ' Shock raced through Alan. Something dreadful must have happened for Clare to contemplate doing this!

'I can come home now. I'll bring the plane to Glasgow Airport, and get a taxi from there,' he said.

'Oh, would you?' Susan sounded relieved. 'She's coming home for the weekend. But if we could talk things over before then, think of how best we can help her . . . '

★ ★ ★

It seemed ages before Susan heard a taxi draw up outside the house. She opened the front door just as Alan reached the house.

They took one look, and moved into one another's arms to stand for a long moment, gaining comfort from the embrace.

Susan relaxed against him.

'Oh, I'm so glad you're here!' She hugged him, relishing the once-familiar haven of Alan's arms.

'Oh, love.' His voice was husky. 'Come on. Let's go and sit down, and you can tell me all about it? What's she done that she's lost heart like this?'

Susan tried to explain how their daughter was feeling.

'She's always been a perfectionist,' Alan said, worried. 'She expects too much of herself — of the whole world.'

'I understand she needs time to think about her future, but she shouldn't be afraid she's letting us down.' Susan was frowning.

'Did we push her into choosing medicine — against her natural inclination?' Alan read her mind.

'We've always talked about pushy parents. Maybe we've turned into them!' Susan shivered a little.

'And now she's suffering because of us.' He took Susan's hand, and her eyes filled with tears.

Support

'Don't cry, love.' He put his arm round her. 'You know we've always tried to do the right thing for all three, and I remember trying to dissuade Clare at one point.

'To be honest, I always thought it would be a hard life for someone like her.'

'I remember you telling her that, but you know how conscientious she's always been . . . and we did say we'd be very proud to have a doctor daughter.' Susan's voice caught on a sob.

'When she comes home, we'll just let her find her feet. We just have to listen, to give her our loving support.'

Their eyes held. Somehow, through this crisis, they'd managed to rediscover the essence of their relationship. They were thinking and speaking as one.

'It's just as well I sent that estate agent packing,' Susan said eventually.

She felt him tense.

'You did?' Alan tried to keep his voice even.

'We can't possibly sell at the moment. Clare needs her own home.' Susan's tone was matter of fact.

'She can have it, at the cottage,' Alan said.

'Away from all her friends? I don't think that would work. She needs time to think, but not in isolation.'

'She won't be isolated,' Alan insisted. 'There will be the three of us, my mother, Gavin at Fearchar — all the folk she knows on the island. Clare always felt safe and at home there.'

'But it's — a step back, into the past.'

Susan leaned back to look at him. 'That's not what she needs. If she decides to give up medicine, Clare will want to look to the future.'

'She can see into the future just as well from Heronsay as anywhere else.' Alan insisted. 'Everyone's future is bound up there now. That's how long it has to be — we really don't have a choice.'

'Alan, this isn't about where we *live*. This is about Clare.'

Alan said nothing. Susan's eyes were full of pain. But he knew how it would have to be in the end. Why wouldn't she recognise it?

'Steve Fixed It'

Jessica's room in one of the Copperhead lodges reminded her of the tiny bedroom she shared with Clare for holidays at Heronsay. Except that the view from the croft cottage didn't include wild grey kangaroos peacefully grazing on the greens of a golf course.

But even the kangaroos couldn't assuage this strange feeling of loneliness. It was early afternoon, and her free shift.

On the very night she'd booked into the Copperhead Hotel, the receptionist had looked at her.

'Are you looking for work? We need staff in the Cappuccino Café.'

The job allowed her to stay on at Copperhead until some flying work came up. Her next shift began at six.

Four hours to fill. Right, time to explore. She picked up a bike from the hire office, and checked in first with Emery at the airfield.

'Hi, Jez,' he greeted her. 'You still here? Nothing for you yet, but if you can stick around I'd like to take you up for a trial flight — as soon as I have a spare plane, of course.'

'You can contact me at the hotel,' she told him. 'I'm working part-time there.'

'No worries.' Emery waved her off.

Jessica had never been off in the

opposite direction from the hotel. The main road was wide and flat, with spectacular views on either side — acres of fields, bordered by bush gently sloping up to the foothills.

She was freewheeling happily when she saw a rider coming towards her.

'Hi, Jez!' Kirralee drew her horse to a halt as Jessica jumped off the bike.

'Great to see you again.' The younger girl beamed down at her. 'How's life at the Cappuccino Café?'

'Good to see you, Kirralee, but how did you know I was working there?'

'Well, Steve fixed it, didn't he?' Then Kirralee clapped her hand to her mouth. 'I wasn't supposed to say anything!'

Had it been anyone else who'd fixed a job for her, Jessica would have been furious. But Steve — now that was different. Was he looking out for her? That felt good.

'Why didn't he want you to say anything?' Jessica wondered.

'He says you're the type who wants

to make it on your own.' Kirralee looked apologetic.

'I am that, but it was good of him. At least the job gives me extra time here to see if I can get some flying work.' Jessica looked up at the empty sky. 'One of the planes is still out of commission, though, and I'm not good at being patient. Time hangs heavy.'

'Come and meet Mum and Dad.' Kirralee nudged the horse round. 'It isn't far.

'Look, there's our spread down there.' She pointed to some low buildings set about half a mile from the main road.

A sign at the road end said *Mac's Trail Riding Centre*. Jessica saw rows of stables, with paddocks behind, and a long low bungalow, with a veranda running all round it, clearly Kirralee's home.

Kirralee trotted towards the house, and a small, wiry woman got up from a chair on the veranda.

'Good on you, Kirralee. You've found

someone!' She smiled at Jessica as her daughter looped her reins round a veranda post.

'Don't rush the fences, Mum.' Kirralee laughed. 'Jez is actually working over at the Copperhead.'

'Really? That must be fun!' Kirralee's mum jumped off the veranda and came over to Jessica. 'Hi, I'm Norelle.'

'Glad to meet you,' Jessica took to Norelle instantly. Bright blue eyes sparkled in tanned skin, and wild, blonde curly hair seemed to make a halo round her head. A cotton plaid shirt flapped over trim khaki shorts.

'Mum's looking for help in the stables.' Kirralee explained. 'Actually, Mum, Jez is a pilot. She's working at Copperhead, but hoping to get some flying work.'

Norelle took a step back from Jessica and surveyed her from head to toe.

'A pilot? It beats me what you young things get up to these days!' She shook her head, eyes twinkling. 'Good on you, Jez.'

'Where's Dad?' Kirralee asked.

'Having a look at Moonbeam — I think he's going to give Steve a call and have him check her over. There he is.'

She pointed, and a little electric thrill raced through Jessica's body as she turned round.

But Norelle hadn't meant Steve. The man over by the stables was of a different build, and older. Jessica couldn't make out his features at this distance, but she reckoned Kirralee took after her father as regarded build and colouring. There was certainly something familiar about his stance.

Jessica stayed for iced tea and cookies.

'You know, you could make some extra money helping out here, if you like,' Norelle said once she'd heard about Jessica's shift work at Copper-head. 'It might help to fill in your off-duty time.'

'Oh, Jez, please,' Kirralee said. 'It would be great to have your company! None of my friends wants to work here in the school holidays.'

Norelle hooted with laughter.

'Now there's a strong recommendation for you!'

Jessica hesitated. She liked both Kirralee and Norelle, typical friendly Australians. It would be good to spend her free time with them, but . . .

'I have to be honest. I don't know my way around horses.'

'The best creatures on God's earth!' Norelle smiled at her. 'We'll teach you all you need to know and love about them.'

It seemed Mac, Kirralee's dad, left all the staffing arrangements to his wife. As Jessica cycled back to the lodge, she was trying to convince herself that she'd soon learn all she needed to know. She was looking forward to it.

And she was bound to see Steve again — he was Mac's vet. A warm curl of hope enveloped her.

This was not the time to dwell on the fact that she was downright scared of horses!

Judith's Guest

'Oh! This is beautiful.' Judith Paton walked into her bedroom at Fearchar.

'It all looks so genuine!' She touched the carving on the bedposts, and moved to examine an old tapestry hung above the writing desk.

'It is genuine.' Gavin smiled, trying to keep the pride from his tone. 'Every single item in Fearchar was acquired by a Lamont at some time during the house's history. So you see, you're in our family home — and we're glad to have you here.'

Judith turned to look at him. When she found he was gazing at her, she gave him a small smile.

Her whole face changed as her eyes smiled, he thought.

'You didn't enjoy the helicopter ride?'

'Well, it was my first time, but it was fine. It just made me think that everything else about this place would be . . . modern.'

'I've just acquired the helicopter,' he

explained. 'Before, our guests, and the islanders, had to travel by boat to Bradan, the next island, then bus over to the ferry port at Fiadh, and on to Oban.

'It's good to cut some of that hassle out. I hope it will improve the quality of life for everyone on Heronsay.'

'I understand now.' She smiled again. 'I made a wrong assumption. I'm really concerned about conservation, you see, so I wondered — '

'As am I,' Gavin said quickly. 'Maybe we could discuss it later? Eileen will be ready to serve lunch in about fifteen minutes.'

'Thank you.'

When she came downstairs, the other guests were already settled at a table for four. Gavin showed her to a table by the other window.

'Do you prefer to eat alone, or may I join you?' he asked.

'Oh, please, sit down.' She looked flustered, as Gavin swiftly laid another place.

She seemed an odd mixture, this girl. Her clothes were smart but not expensive, and that led him to think a place like Fearchar wouldn't be her usual choice for a holiday.

She might feel less nervous with company.

'Now tell me what aspect of conservation you're interested in,' he said once they'd finished the soup.

'Flowers,' she said at once. 'I'm writing and illustrating a book on endangered species of wild flowers and plants.'

'You think you might find some here on Heronsay?' Gavin was surprised.

'I hope to. You haven't had anyone here before doing research?' Her eyes were eager, and she seemed pleased when Gavin shook his head.

Judith leaned back in her chair.

'Most of the other Hebridean islands have been written about. It would mean so much if I could make my name with this book!'

'Heronsay isn't very big,' he said gently.

'No, but the terrain is interesting. I noticed that from the air,' she commented. 'Would it be all right if I looked around?'

'Of course. I'd like to help — may I arrange transport?'

'Oh, no! It's so much easier to spot things if you walk.'

'But can you carry your easel around with you?'

'I won't need that until I've found something. Sketches first.'

'I'd be really thrilled if you found something unusual on Heronsay,' he told her.

'So would I!' And she gave him a wide smile, which he found very attractive.

Helping Eileen clear away, he told her about Judith's plans.

'Mystery solved,' she said. 'I didn't think she was our normal kind of guest. She has the look of someone who has a job to do, rather than enjoy leisure time.

'She'll certainly have her work cut out here.'

'What you do mean?' Gavin asked.

'She's only booked in for three days. She can hardly draw every flower on the island in that time!'

Gavin returned to his office, deep in thought. A successful book would be good not only for Judith Paton, but also for Heronsay.

But Eileen had a point. Was three days at Fearchar all Judith could afford?

He'd have to think this over . . .

★   ★   ★

Clare was about to switch off her computer before going to Glasgow for the weekend when she found an e-mail from her sister.

It was in typical Jessica style. Now that she was away from Brisbane, she couldn't afford to phone, so reading the e-mail was just like listening to her sister.

Clare, I need to know everything!

I'm so upset that you're thinking of giving up your course. I mean, I'm upset because I don't know the reasons! What can I do? Shall I come home, so that we can talk one-to-one on this?

I know it's not easy talking to the parents — different generation and all that, and they have expectations (well, not of me, I suspect).

Or would you like to come out here for a couple of months? Dad must be loaded with all that redundancy money — I'm sure he would give you the fare.

For the first time ever I feel so far away from you. Please let me help.

Love, Jessica.

Clare printed out the message, switched off the computer and put the sheet of paper in her bag. Mum had obviously told Jessica.

For a moment she longed to be beside her sister, listening to Jessica rant on about something, anything.

No, rant was too strong a word. It was just that Jessica was so passionate about everything she undertook. She could phone Jessica from home and try to reassure her . . . Then, once again, the sinking feeling came over her. She just didn't know what to do.

'Clare!' There was a knock on the door.

'It's Will for you,' her flatmate called.

Clare picked up her weekend bag and went downstairs. Will was in the hall, a bag slung over his shoulder.

'OK if I come with you?' he said casually. 'I called your parents and booked a room in the hope you'd say 'yes'.'

As always when she looked at Will, Clare's heart turned over. She knew she wanted him by her side for ever, but now it mightn't work out that way. And she had so hoped to discuss her problems with her parents on her own . . .

But Will's long face was creased with concern, and she slipped her arm through his.

'Sure,' she said.

As they left the flat, Clare felt hollow

guilt stealing over her again.

She was surrounded by love and care from Will, and Jessica was obviously concerned. But somehow, she couldn't explain to anyone exactly how she felt.

The Big Picture

'Eileen! Lovely to hear you again.' Susan dropped into a chair.

'Sorry I didn't call you back. I needed Alan because Clare's coming home this weekend. She's distressed over something to do with her course . . . I can't say any more at this stage.'

'I could tell you were upset over something,' her mother-in-law's warm voice said. 'I thought it might have been the business of the cottage?'

There was silence.

'I haven't even begun to think about that.' Susan rubbed her forehead. 'I've just sent Alan out for groceries — Will's coming with Clare, and you know how he eats.'

'Is it what you want, my dear, to come to Heronsay to live?' Eileen had always been close to Susan and straight talking was part of that relationship.

'No, it isn't,' Susan said grimly. 'I know Alan genuinely thinks it's for the best, but it's liable to start all sorts of problems if we have to leave Glasgow.'

'Well, there's your course, for a start. You can't give that up.' Eileen sounded so decisive that Susan almost wanted to cheer. Somebody saw it her way!

'My wishes are only part of it. I wish Alan could see the big picture.'

'I've been thinking along those lines, too. If I can help, I will,' Eileen said. 'I don't want you two going head to head on this.

'I can see both sides of the problem. The trouble is, my loyalties are divided.'

'We don't want to put you in a difficult position,' Susan said immediately. 'It's just that . . . well, I might need a sympathetic ear from time to time.'

'You always have that,' Eileen assured her.

'I know. I'll let you know about Clare after the weekend,' Susan promised.

★　★　★

'They're an unlikely couple, aren't they?' Susan said, looking out of the living-room window as Clare and Will shut car doors and took bags out.

'Yeah. She's so neat and composed, he's tall and gangly and it goes for their personalities, too.'

'Oh, yes,' Susan agreed. 'He's the complete extrovert. You'd never guess his parents were missionaries!'

Alan laughed at that.

'Medical missionaries, though.'

Will had brought out hidden aspects of Clare's personality, made her laugh, and clearly cared for her. She was in safe hands, Susan knew.

'I'm starving,' Will announced once

91

greetings were over. 'So I'm going to inflict some American cooking on you all.'

'Is that why I had to buy all those strange ingredients?' Alan teased.

'Exactly. I'm cooking the meal while you have time with Clare.' He gave them a casual smile and disappeared into the kitchen.

So tactful. Alan and Susan exchanged a grateful smile, and Clare felt even worse.

Everyone was being thoughtful and caring, but she didn't deserve it. She didn't want to talk, only crawl away into a room somewhere, quite alone, and try to think out what she should do with her life.

'I can't tell you what's wrong. I just know I've done the wrong thing choosing medicine.' She looked squarely at her parents.

'Maybe *you* didn't do the wrong thing, Clare. Mum and I have been thinking back to when we discussed your university choices. We could have pushed you into it,' her father said.

'Oh, no, nothing like that!' They were trying to blame themselves!

'You know I've always talked about being a doctor, since I was little. Now I know the reality, and it's different.'

She paused, but she could see they were still worried.

'Then there's this Africa thing. You know Will's uncle's an eye surgeon in the States?

'Well, he's flying out to the mission in Africa to treat people — from the plane. We've both been asked out for the vacation — to help, but also learn.'

'And Will wants to go?' Susan asked.

Clare nodded.

'And you don't?' Alan said gently.

'Yes, I do.' She paused. 'Did. It's exactly the area of medicine that appeals to me, but I can't do it. I'm terrified I'll let everyone down, especially Will.'

She felt her voice going again, and her mother took her hand.

'Then you mustn't go,' Susan said quietly. 'Maybe it's too soon, perhaps you need time to take stock.

'Darling, we want to help. Just tell us how to do it.'

'Would you like a spell on Heronsay, at the cottage?' Alan offered, and Clare thought for a moment.

She wasn't even ready for that, but Dad looked so hopeful.

'Maybe — later,' she said.

'A visit to Jessica?' Susan suggested, and Clare summoned a smile.

'I got this e-mail from her. She wants to see me, but, honestly, Mum, I'd drive her nuts. We're so different . . . '

There was a long silence in the room.

'Maybe you'd just like to be entirely on your own?' Susan said.

Mum always understood. Clare felt tears rushing to her eyes.

Susan came and put her arm round Clare's shoulder.

'Just keep going until the end of

94

term, keep your spirits up for Will. And then — as much privacy as you want,' she said in Clare's ear. 'I'll just go and check if the feast is ready.'

Daniel's News

Susan's striped cook's apron barely covered Will's chest. He was almost ready to serve the meal.

He raised his eyebrows as Susan came in.

'Time alone,' she said.

'I guessed as much.' He shook his head. 'I'll be away for six weeks, and I wish she was coming. I'm gonna miss her like crazy, but I'd rather that than lose Clare for the rest of my life.'

'That's true love,' Susan said lightly. 'Shall I take this salad through? You look all ready to dish up.'

They carried the meal into the dining-room, and were just about to begin when Daniel rushed in.

'Hey, you weren't going to start

without me?' he demanded. 'Is there enough food for me?'

'There's enough for the entire state of Missouri,' Will said calmly.

Daniel eyed the table.

'Well, they can't eat much, that's all I can say.' Daniel puffed out his chest. 'I need to build up my strength.'

Nobody said anything.

'Well, ask me!'

'Sounds like a big moment,' Will said.

'I've just been chosen for next year's football team! You know I've been trying for ages, Dad. It was the final trials today. And I'm in!'

'That's great!' Clare grinned at her brother, but Susan glanced across the table at Alan. He wouldn't meet her eyes.

'So, Dad,' Daniel went on, 'Gavin will have to give you every Saturday off so that you can fly over to see me play.

'Practice is Wednesday night, right in the middle of the week, so I'll have to stay in Glasgow over the winter.'

Alan looked up at last, pleadingly, at

Susan, who stared back at him. This was entirely his problem. She wasn't going to be the one who crushed all Daniel's pride and hopes.

Intrigued

Gavin had never expected Judith Paton to haunt him, sleeping and waking, but he found it impossible to think of anyone or anything else.

It had been a wonderful evening. All the guests had been so relaxed, and there had been lots of laughter and daft jokes.

But the best part for Gavin was listening to Judith.

She was wearing a soft flowing dress of crushed velvet, its delicate coral colour highlighting her complexion.

'I taught in Kirkcudbrightshire for ten years.' She was replying to a question from one of the other guests.

'Then an inheritance . . . ' She paused. 'At last I had funds to tackle my book.'

She turned to Gavin with that brilliant smile.

'I have to tell you — I found an orchid today.'

'An orchid? Here on Heronsay?'

'Oh, it's not the rarest, but who knows? I may find something more special tomorrow.'

Gavin nodded. Ever since she had stepped off the helicopter he'd been intrigued by her. Was it due to that smile? The vulnerable expression in those soft blue eyes? Or could it be the gentle tone of her voice?

Abruptly, Gavin rose to fetch more coffee. Goodness, she'd scarcely been on Heronsay for twenty-four hours. He couldn't sit there embarrassing her!

Despite his resolve to keep a little distance between them, when she didn't rush upstairs with the other guests, he changed his mind.

'How long will it take you to find everything you're looking for on Heronsay?' he asked, throwing another log on the fire.

When he looked at her, she was twisting the stem of her wine glass, gazing into the depths of the wine.

'Longer than I thought,' she said finally.

'Stay at Fearchar as long as you like.' The words tumbled out eagerly before Gavin could stop them, but she looked away.

'I'd like to . . . but it might be difficult.'

'We can come to some arrangement . . . ' he began clumsily, anxious to keep her on Heronsay.

'It isn't quite as easy as that, Gavin.'

He was so thrilled to hear her using his first name that he nearly missed the next bit.

'The legacy was from my father,' she said quietly. 'I stayed with him during his last illness, and he planned the legacy so that I could take a sabbatical from school and write the book I've always planned.'

'He knew all about it, then?'

Judith nodded.

'He was a wonderful gardener, until his last few years. He taught me so much, about plants, and habitats, and cultivation.'

There was a little silence.

'So the legacy has to support you until the book's done.'

She looked up, a gleam of grateful understanding in her eyes.

'Exactly. And I have to use it properly . . . for him.'

★ ★ ★

Gavin was furious when he drew back his curtains next morning and saw the downpour outside.

Of all days, just when Judith had accepted his offer to drive her round the island! He so much wanted to show her it at its best.

The last thing he wanted was for her work on Heronsay to be finished, but he would have her company for a whole day . . . and perhaps have a chance to explain his brilliant solution to keep her here a little longer.

The rain proved to be a blessing. Armed with her map, Judith directed Gavin to the places where she thought she might find interesting plants.

Finding them meant dashing out into the rain, cowering together under the golf umbrella, then returning to the Land-Rover for a hot drink before moving on to the next site.

You couldn't be stand-offish after a morning spent like that. They laughed and joked, and mopped splashes of mud from each other's faces.

Gavin didn't think it remotely possible that Judith could be interested in him, but by the end of the afternoon he knew one thing for certain. He'd fallen in love.

Yet he was conscious he had to be careful. The last thing he wanted to do was rush things.

'Gavin, I can't thank you enough,' she said when they finally arrived back at Fearchar. 'You've been a perfect companion, and really helped me with everything.'

Perfect companion. Well, it was a start!

Over dinner, he broached his plan.

'Have you noticed that there's an empty cottage behind Fearchar?'

'Oh, yes, I can see it from my bedroom window. I didn't realise it was empty,' she said. But then she realised what he meant.

'It belongs to Eileen,' he began.

'But Eileen lives in here at Fearchar, doesn't she?'

'Shall I ask her if you could rent it?'

'Oh Gavin, that would be wonderful! I do need to have much more time here. Today proved that — there's so much to do.'

'Leave it to me.'

Gavin knew, of course, that Alan was planning to move into the cottage, but surely that couldn't be for months yet? After all, they still had the Glasgow house!

Judith was smiling, in a way he

hadn't seen before. For the first time, there was more than gratitude in her eyes. He didn't dare hope — not yet.

A Visit From Steve

'Oh, Jessica, you do exaggerate at times!' Her mother's words echoed in her ears as Jessica woke, and she found them comforting.

This was her first day helping out at Mac's Trail Riding Centre, and she was determined to cope. After all, what were horses? Just big soft creatures that munched away in fields and did what they were told.

'So, no big deal,' she told the kookaburra in the tree outside the lodge. It obligingly woke Jessica at dawn every day, and her body clock had adjusted to the five a.m. call.

Last night she'd had a long phone chat with Clare, and it had been such a relief to talk to her sister.

'I miss you, of course, Jess, but

what could you do if you came home? No more than Mum and Dad are already doing. You stay where you are and enjoy it.

'And keep e-mailing — your e-mails are my lifeline!' Clare laughed.

Jessica had been prepared to do anything to help, but she was relieved that she didn't have to leave Queensland. Life was just so good out here.

On that thought she scrambled out of bed.

It was a quiet morning at the centre, a good opportunity, Norelle said, to catch up on all the jobs waiting to be done.

'Kirralee's gone on a school trip, and Mac's away looking at some horses. So it's just the two of us.'

Armed with a pitchfork, rake and wheelbarrow, Jessica set about mucking out, Norelle throwing instructions over her shoulder from time to time.

'Good work, Jez!' she said when they stopped for a break. 'I could do with you around full time, and we have a spare room. Like to think about it?'

'Thanks, Norelle, but maybe I'd better keep my options open. I've put my name down at the airfield for relief pilot, remember.'

'Oh, I forgot about that! You can still bunk here if you like, though. Oh, drat, that's my phone ringing back at the house. Back in just a jiffy.'

Jessica rubbed her back, a little stiff after all the physical work.

Norelle still hadn't returned when she heard a vehicle approaching and she straightened up.

It might be Mac. She still hadn't spoken to Kirralee's dad, only glimpsed him in the distance.

He'd had an accident years ago, Kirralee told her. It had left him with a badly-damaged knee, but that didn't matter once he was on a horse.

'He's an ace rider.' Kirralee explained, 'but walking's difficult, and that frustrates him.'

Then Jessica saw who was climbing down from the ute, and her heart skipped a couple of beats.

Steve! She tried to keep her intense pleasure at seeing him off her face. But she needn't have worried — he was talking to someone inside the ute.

Then he turned his head and caught sight of her.

'Jez! Hi!' he called. 'Come and see what I've got here!'

When she reached him, he was carefully lifting out a bundle, wrapped up like a baby in swaddling clothes.

'Here. What do you think of this?' He held it out.

A huge pair of brown eyes stared up at her. The animal was nestled in an old sweatshirt.

'It's a baby!' Jessica cried. 'But a baby what?'

'Wallaby. Just a joey,' Steve said. 'Found him by the roadside. He's lost his mother.'

'Oh, the poor little thing!'

'Here, hold him a minute while I get my bag.' Steve put the bundle in Jessica's arms, and she cradled it as it trembled against her.

'Where's the mother gone?'

'Doubt if I'll find her.' Steve shook his head. 'She might have been in an accident, or been attacked by a dingo.'

'Oh, no!' Tears came to her eyes, and Steve immediately put a comforting hand on her shoulder.

'Hey, Jez, don't take on so. This is the wild — things like this happen. You must know that from your Scottish countryside.'

She nodded, talking softly to the joey and stroking his head with a gentle finger.

'What will happen to him?'

'I'll look after him until he's ready to go back out on his own. I reckon he was about to leave his mother's pouch for good, anyway.' He smiled at her.

'Like to go on nursing him for a bit? I've just got to check up on Moonbeam's leg.'

Kirralee's horse stood patiently while Steve attended to her.

'Thanks for putting in a word for me

at Copperhead,' she said.

'Thought you might need something until a flying option came up,' he said casually.

'I haven't heard anything from Emery at the charter company, so I expect the plane is still grounded. But at least I've got two jobs and a bed, in the meantime.'

'A job here, too?' he asked.

She nodded.

Steve patted Moonbeam's head.

'You'll be OK now, girl. We'll take her out to the paddock.'

The Perfect Job

Together they walked over from the stables. 'I guess you're game to tackle anything?' he said casually.

'There's a heap of things in this world I haven't tried yet!' She laughed, at ease in his company.

'Like to work for me for a couple of weeks?'

The question took her completely by surprise.

Being near Steve every day for two weeks! Jessica was thrilled for a moment, before commonsense asserted itself.

'I know very little about animals. I could be a disaster,' she warned, and Steve threw his head back, laughing.

'You could never be a disaster, Jez. I reckon you can handle most things. And you like a challenge.'

He fastened the paddock gate, and stroked the joey's head.

'I need someone to make appointments, keep the records up to date, that kind of thing, just for two weeks. A couple of hours a day should cover it.' He raised his eyebrows.

'I wouldn't have to help with operations, and things?'

'No way. I wouldn't throw that at you. I'm training a vet assistant, and we'll handle all the medical stuff.

'You could talk to the recuperating animals. I guess they'd like that — like this fella!'

In a daze, Jessica said she'd love to do the job.

They put the joey back in his nest in the ute and went to find Norelle.

'That call was for you, Jez. I looked out and saw you were taking Steve over, or I'd have got you to the phone.

'The plane's fixed, and Emery wants to take you up for that trial flight.'

'Oh, gosh! I'd better go right now.' Jessica gasped. 'I'm due back at Copperhead in a couple of hours.'

'Don't forget you're due back with me in two weeks' time,' Steve reminded her.

'Don't worry, I won't let you down,' she promised, with her best smile.

Life, she thought, biking to the airfield, surely could not get any better than this.

Dan In Trouble

'Thanks. We'll stay in touch.'

Alan closed the door behind the

110

estate agent. He'd arranged this visit deliberately while Susan was at college and Daniel at school. Clare was shopping in town.

He knew the family would react very emotionally to the thought of their home belonging to other people, and he wanted to spare them that as long as possible.

But he needed to sell soon. No point in paying interest unnecessarily.

And the house had got a better valuation than Alan had expected. There would be cash left over for some treats, over and above the money he needed for Heronsay.

Once the family understood how many benefits Ingram Air would bring to their lives, they'd soon adjust to leaving Glasgow.

He was humming under his breath when the phone rang. It was the secretary at Daniel's school.

'Mr Ingram? I wonder if you and Mrs Ingram would be free to come in today to see Mr Steadman? It's about

Daniel, and it's rather urgent. A disciplinary matter.'

Alan was taken aback.

'Of course. I'll get in touch with my wife right away.'

★ ★ ★

'What's he done?' Susan's voice was tight with anxiety as she abandoned her car inside the school gates and rushed to join Alan.

'They didn't say on the phone.' He put an arm round her. 'Come on, love, don't get upset. We'll soon find out.'

He sounded much more positive than he felt.

'It isn't what Daniel's done.' Mr Steadman explained as they sat down. 'Rather what he hasn't done.

'The work in these books is appalling. His homework hasn't been completed at all for two weeks now, and when he's reprimanded, he just shrugs.'

The head looked at them.

'Daniel's been an excellent pupil

until now, and I know it's near the end of term, but we have to get to the bottom of this.'

'Daniel has told you that we're leaving Glasgow?' Susan said. 'He was supposed to let you know.'

'Not a word.' The head sat up. 'Where are you taking him?'

'I took early redundancy, and I've gone into business with a colleague on the island of Heronsay. We have to move there,' Alan explained.

'And Daniel doesn't want to go.' The head understood at once.

'I know it's really tough on him, especially now he's made the team. The irony of it is that I thought, living on Heronsay, Daniel and I would have much more time together.' Alan paused. 'While I was on long-haul flights, I didn't see very much of my son.'

'I do understand, Mr Ingram.' The head thought for a moment. 'In the circumstances, I won't discipline Daniel too severely, but we'll have to work on this, for his sake.'

'It's our fault.' Susan said at once. 'We've never sat down and let him talk to us about all this. The way he found out — '

'Yes, well.' Alan interrupted. He didn't want to think about the look in Dan's eyes when he realised he couldn't take up his place in the team, because he wouldn't be there any more. 'We'll sort this out. I promise.'

'Easy enough to say,' Susan remarked, back at home. 'We've been treating Dan like the girls, as if he were a grown-up, too.'

'Do you remember the time he went to bed wearing his entire school uniform under his pyjamas, so he wouldn't have to get up so early in the morning?' Alan said, and Susan laughed shakily.

'I'd forgotten that. It was so funny. I wish you'd been at home to see it.'

'I've entertained so many of my crews with that story. And that's been half the trouble — I haven't been around to share things with him. He

114

hasn't understood that's all going to change.'

'That's only part of it, Alan. I've neglected him — not deliberately, but thinking he could cope with all the turmoil of leaving school, not making time to listen to his worries ...'

Alan took her in his arms.

'And we've been arguing. Perhaps he thinks we don't care any more, not only about him, but for each other. That can affect children very badly.' He kissed her hair.

'My darling, many things are going to change, but one thing never will — my love for you.'

She hugged him closer.

'Oh, Alan, I've been so afraid we've been drifting apart, and I don't want that. We may never go back to the rapture that brought us together, but I love you so much!'

'That's all I needed to hear,' he whispered into her hair. 'It's going to be tough, but we'll get through this together.'

They decided to take Daniel out for a meal so that they could discuss things on neutral territory.

The moment he got into the car, they could see the head had spoken to him. But it wasn't until their meal had been served that Alan said anything.

'This is my fault, Dan. If I'd had any idea that leaving the airline would cause all this upset, I'd have thought twice.'

Daniel looked at him.

'But I would still have come to the same decision,' Alan went on.

'Because by doing this, I'll see more of you.'

He saw a flash of surprise in his son's eyes. So they'd been right. Dan had no idea what had been behind their decision.

'Mr Steadman said that.' Daniel's eyes were on his food again. 'He said I might find my father was more important than my football team.'

'Did he?' Susan grinned at him. 'It's a pity you're leaving him behind. He's good, Mr Steadman.'

'Yeah,' Daniel agreed huskily.

'Not to worry, Dan.' Alan's voice was gentle. 'But there will be a new school, on Bradan, probably, come the autumn, so you'll have to make up for lost time. OK?'

'The girls have been lucky.' Susan broke in, seeing her tough wee boy near to tears. 'They didn't have to move away from friends and school . . .

'We know it won't be easy, Dan, but you've got the guts to handle it.'

'And you know we're behind you all the way, just as Mum and I are for each other,' Alan added.

Daniel shrugged and ate a mouthful of burger.

It still wasn't going to be plain sailing, Alan thought, but at least they'd made a start . . .

★ ★ ★

'Thanks, Mum. See you later!' Clare waved as she drove Mum's car off down the road. It wasn't far to

Gran's, but since she was taking so much stuff with her, Mum had lent her the car.

Clare had pretended it was just clothes, CDs and books, but she'd also packed some course notes.

Somehow she just couldn't leave it alone. She knew she wanted to drop out of the course, but the subject continued to fascinate her. Of course, the theory wasn't the problem, just the practice.

There would be peace at Gran's, to study or to think. And if Gran hadn't come to dinner that night, during the upset with Daniel, Clare wouldn't have got the chance.

The tension was plain to everyone round the table. Dan wasn't sulking, as such, but he was monosyllabic, and Mum was much too bright.

It was a relief when Dan was doing his homework upstairs and the rest were having coffee.

Gran's New Friend

'Do you remember I told you I'm taking my language group to France?' Gran said.

'Yes. You should have fun with that.' Susan smiled at her mother.

'Oh, we'll all have fun.' Marion set down her coffee cup. 'It's just — I'm rather concerned about leaving my flat empty.

'Maybe you'd like to flat-sit for me, Clare, if it wouldn't be too much of a bore?'

Clare knew instinctively Gran was offering her a refuge, and jumped at the chance.

As she drew up at the block of flats overlooking Bellahouston Park, Clare felt some of the tension drain from her. Being completely alone might help. After all, nobody else could make this decision for her.

She was getting out of the car when Gran appeared, with a man Clare hadn't met before.

'Hello, love. Thank you for doing this!' Gran kissed her cheek.

'Clare, this is my friend, Harry, who's coming on the trip with me. He'll help carry your stuff upstairs.'

'I'm Harry Macmillan. Good to meet you, Clare.' Harry's smile lit up his lined, friendly face. Silver-grey hair, thinning a little, made a good contrast with his clear blue eyes.

'Hello, and thank you.' Clare gestured at the open boot. 'I seem to have brought enough stuff for a siege!' She grinned.

'Looks like it!' Marion laughed.

'And your gran's left enough food for you, should there *be* a siege!' Harry took her big backpack across the hall to the lift.

Inside the flat, they had a quick cup of tea while Gran ran over her little list about the flat. Clare listened attentively, but all the time her mind was busy.

Why hadn't they heard about Harry Macmillan before? He and Gran seemed comfortable in each other's company, and she noticed how he helped out unobtrusively, just to make things easier for her.

Extra Sparkle

'We're going to collect two other members of our group, and then it's off to Glasgow Airport.' Gran smiled. 'Now, you will be fine on your own?'

'Go, and have a lovely time.' Clare hugged her.

'I don't know about that. She expects us all to do the talking in France — in French!' Harry grumbled, but his look at Gran was affectionate.

Clare waved from the window as they drove off. There was no doubt about it, Gran had an extra sparkle today.

'Would you believe it?' Clare said aloud, delighted. 'Good on you, Gran!'

Looking back, Clare reckoned it must have been fifteen years ago that they lost Grandad. Gran must have been pretty lonely sometimes.

It wasn't long before Clare came to know about loneliness herself.

Her time in the flat began well — she did exactly what she wanted, when she wanted to. She even enjoyed burying herself in her medical studies again.

Phone calls to Will and Jessica were reassuring — she missed them both so much — but she would have enjoyed sharing a meal with someone. Trouble was, most of her Glasgow pals were off on holiday jobs or actually on holiday.

So the phone call from Heronsay was a delightful surprise.

'Laurie! Gosh, am I glad to hear from you. We haven't spoken for too long!'

Clare and Laurie had been close friends all through her childhood holidays on Heronsay, and they'd kept in touch; she'd been at Laurie's island wedding.

'I'll say!' Laurie chuckled. 'And if you don't visit me soon, you'll be pram-pushing next time I see you.'

'A baby! Oh, Laurie, I'm thrilled for you,' Clare said.

'How about coming to see me before the big event?' Laurie asked. 'Word on the island is your family's moving here anyway. Will you be coming with them?'

'Not settled yet.' Clare didn't know herself where she'd be, come the autumn. 'But I'd really like to see you soon.'

'Great,' Laurie replied. 'Pete goes back on the rig in a couple of weeks' time, so some time after then?'

When she hung up, Clare put on the kettle for a hot drink, feeling happier than at any time since she'd left Edinburgh.

Something to look forward to — staying with Laurie, and sharing her excitement about the baby!

A Shock For Susan

It was early on Saturday morning when Eileen phoned Glasgow. She got Susan.

'One of Gavin's guests wants to rent the cottage for a while. She's writing a book and needs more time here, but Fearchar's fully booked for the next few weeks.

'I've agreed to it — better than the place lying empty — but is that OK with you?'

'Yes, fine. We haven't done anything about selling the house here yet.

'Anyway, you can discuss it with Alan. He and Daniel are flying up this morning — should be with you soon.'

'Daniel, too? Oh, how marvellous! I'd better order in extra food. That boy invented hollow legs!' Daniel's gran laughed.

Alan and Daniel had departed at some unearthly hour. Susan had the whole day to herself, and planned to work on her design project.

She'd just come out of the shower when she heard banging outside the house. When she opened the front door, an estate agent's *For Sale* board was facing her.

'Just a minute!' she called to the man shutting the doors of a van. 'Who authorised this sign?'

'I just take orders from the office, madam. I have a location note here.' He showed her a typed list of properties. It came as no surprise to see Alan's name opposite their address.

Her heart lurched sickeningly. How could he have done this without telling her?

Only last night, they had sat down and discussed the financial situation in detail, and she'd accepted that the sale of the house would be necessary eventually.

'I want to extend the cottage, and I need to build a hangar,' he explained. 'That will take a good deal of cash.'

'Well, how about this?' Susan had been confident they were still working together. 'What about selling the house to a letting agency, then renting it ourselves, just for the year?'

Alan mulled over her suggestion.

'I just feel that might make things more complicated financially. And besides, we wouldn't be all together.'

'It would only be temporary — and it would allow Daniel to have his place in the football team.'

'And then there's your course to consider.' There was an edge to Alan's tone.

'That, too.'

Alan gathered up the papers in front of him.

'If that's so important, why don't you just stay with your mother for a year?'

Listening to him stamping upstairs, Susan reflected on how Alan would react to the news she'd considered that very option.

She'd almost decided to suggest it once Mum was back from France. But then Clare had phoned for a chat, and mentioned Harry Macmillan, and how happy Gran was . . .

Susan had been delighted for Mum, who'd had so much heartache after losing Dad on top of the other awful split in the family.

Mum still couldn't talk about that. The last thing she needed was Ingram family problems on her doorstep, plus members of the family living with her!

That *For Sale* sign was like a betrayal. Alan must have had the house valued before he advertised it for sale.

How could he? Had his words of love been empty of meaning? Did her feelings mean so little to him?

She felt cold, first of all with heartache, then with anger. She'd been ready to give up her course to fulfil Alan's dreams and to keep them together.

Well, forget that! Where was that application form? Summer school in Somerset sounded just what she needed.

She'd just stamped the envelope when the phone rang. She glared at it, then slammed the front door behind her and marched off to the post box.

Daniel's Ambitions

'Have you checked the tides, Dad?' Daniel sat in the co-pilot's seat, studying the instrumental panel of

IngramAir's one aircraft. All around the plane stretched the firm sands of Claddach beach.

Alan concealed a smile.

'Sure have, though this is a safe beach, perfect for a runway.'

Daniel began to work his way through the pre-flight checks.

'How am I doing, Dad?'

'Great! You've remembered every-thing. I'd take you on as co-pilot any day. Right, ready for take-off?'

The plane picked up speed along the beach, and soon they were airborne.

'Gosh, this is so cool.' Daniel looked out of the window.

Alan banked the jet and set a course to fly over Bradan while Daniel chattered on.

'What subjects should I concentrate on at school to help me be a pilot?'

'Maths and physics, for a start.'

Daniel's enthusiasm was high at the moment, but there was a long hard road to becoming a pilot, and it paid to be cautious.

'Is that Bradan School down here?' Daniel pointed.

This was the tricky bit. It was a terrible wrench for Dan to leave his Glasgow school. Alan needed to be straight with him about the move.

'That's right, and I have to say it looks better than when I was there! See the new swimming-pool?

'I'm not going to pretend that it'll be like your present school, Dan. There will be a lot of differences and, besides, you'll have to make new friends.'

'I know. But you'll be around to help me.' Dan sounded unconcerned.

Alan knew that the excitement of flying in the new plane had made his son forget for a moment all he would be leaving behind.

'And you'll be flying me back and forth to school.' Dan was still gazing out of the window.

'Only if Uncle Gavin doesn't need the helicopter. There's no landing strip on Bradan, but we have permission to use their helipad there.'

'Cool!'

'OK — let's run over the details for landing.'

Minutes later the plane touched down smoothly on the beach.

'Where are you going to build the hangar?' Dan asked as they walked up the sand, and Alan pointed it out.

'Should be a good foundation there, but I'll have to check with Uncle Gavin. It's his land.'

'I reckon it's not going to be so bad living on Heronsay, after all!' They were heading for Fearchar now.

'It will be great, you'll see. Anyway, you can have the big bedroom at the cottage, the one the girls used to share. They won't be coming to live here again, just visiting.'

'Great. Can I have my own TV in it?'

'One thing at a time.' Alan laughed.

At the big house, Eileen told them Gavin was over at the cottage with Judith Paton.

'Whatever for?' Alan said blankly.

'She wants to rent it,' Eileen said.

'Out of the question. We'll be moving in soon!'

'But Susan said it won't be for a while.' His mother looked worried.

'When did she say that?'

'This morning — I rang her just to check,' Eileen said. 'You'd already left home.'

Alan said nothing. He couldn't involve his mother in the tug of war he and Susan were engaged in. But he had to stop Gavin's guest from renting their new home!

A Bombshell

'Good — here's Alan now. We can sort out your tenancy, Judith.' Gavin smiled as he watched Alan and Dan approaching.

Somehow, Gavin thought, Alan's body language seemed to have nothing to do with what Dan was saying. He and Alan had grown up together, and could read each other like books.

Alan's long stride was full of determination. At a guess, he didn't agree with his mother about Judith renting the cottage.

'Judith! How nice to see you again.'

Gavin was also quietly amused when Alan turned on the charm. Alan could be very persuasive when he wanted something.

Unaware of any undercurrents, Judith immediately bubbled over with enthusiasm.

'I can't tell you how grateful I feel being able to rent your cottage! There's far more work to do than I thought.

'Heronsay's a fabulous place, and it will be wonderful if my book can show that to the rest of the world.'

Alan looked at her sparkling eyes, and his indignation melted.

'I've lived here off and on my whole life, Judith. It would be great if your book put Heronsay on the map.

'It would be a fairly short-term let, mind,' he added. 'We don't have a date to flit from Glasgow yet.'

'That's what I thought,' Gavin said. 'Besides, you have quite a bit of work to do before you settle in.'

'That's true — we need to build an extension on the cottage. We need office space to run IngramAir, apart from anything else.' Alan turned to Judith. 'The building work won't disturb you — it'll be on the other side of the house.'

'Oh, no! Not where the orchid's growing?' Judith cast an anxious look at Gavin.

'Orchid? Here on Heronsay? You have to be joking.' Alan laughed.

'Not at all,' Gavin held his eyes. 'There's a rare species round the side of the house and Judith reckons it's been there for years, so it should be protected.

'I suppose that's why the hill behind the cottage is called Balderry — old Scots for wild orchid.'

'Can I see this specimen?' Alan's easy charm had slipped a little.

The three of them walked round the

cottage. Daniel, bored, had wandered off up the hill.

'Look!' Judith's eyes were bright. 'It's one of the marsh orchid family but I haven't identified it yet. It doesn't always flower every year, so it's pretty special.'

Judith knelt to caress the insignificant green stems with her fingertip.

'It's bound to be a first for Heronsay. Even the Inner Hebrides, if we're lucky!' Gavin sounded just as keen.

'And, Alan, it's a marsh orchid. Bog, right? Not too good for foundations? But you hadn't got the length of an architect, had you?'

He smiled inwardly as he recognised Alan's familiar sulk mode.

'We'll think of some other way to build on. I won't put up any objections.'

He turned to smile at Judith again. If Alan had been looking, he would have been stunned at the expression in his old friend's eyes.

★ ★ ★

'Here we are, folks!' The coach deposited Marion's party at their hotel in the Avenue de Clichy. She'd brought innumerable school trips to Paris over the years, and the city never failed to excite her.

Somehow, it was even better having Harry with her. When he first joined her French class, Marion had assumed he wanted to keep his brain active, like all retired folk.

Gradually, as the group discussed all sorts of things, she'd found she and Harry shared many interests — music, painting, buildings. It had been amusing to have someone to take her along to a concert or a gallery.

'You were absolutely right,' Harry murmured in her ear, as the driver unloaded their suitcases.

He was admiring the buildings on the Avenue.

'You ain't seen nothing yet!' she said jokingly. 'Wait till you see the churches — and there's Versailles tomorrow.'

That evening, the whole party took a *bateau mouche* trip along the Seine, serenaded by musicians.

'This is very romantic, for an old codger like me,' Harry whispered in her ear, and Marion laughed.

'*En Français*,' she reminded him.

'Not tonight. I can only be romantic in my own language!' He took her arm.

He was looking at her warily, she saw, as if he might have overstepped the mark, and she squeezed his arm to reassure him.

Harry's Secret

It was next morning, over breakfast, when Harry dropped his bombshell.

'I'm sorry, but I'll have to skip the visit to Versailles.' He gave Marion an apologetic smile.

'But it's one of the highlights of the trip!' She stared at him in dismay.

'I know, but something's come up. I

didn't plan to do this today, but I can't bear to put it off any longer.'

'I didn't know you had anything arranged while we were here.' She tried to hide her disappointment, but it didn't work.

'I'm sorry, Marion.' He leaned closer. 'I wasn't sure if this would happen — but it's the reason I've been learning French. I can't explain, not yet.'

As he left the dining-room, Marion pulled herself together.

'*Eh bien, mes amis* — Versailles.'

She outlined the visit to her group on automatic pilot.

For some obscure reason she felt let down, though commonsense told her that Harry was not a deceitful person. But if this trip of his was the reason he'd been learning French, why had he never mentioned it?

The rest of the group loved Louis XIV's château — she made sure they did. But as she checked the coach and climbed the hotel steps at the end of the day, she was bone weary.

The first person she saw in the foyer was Harry.

'Please come and have a drink with me before dinner! I've something wonderful to tell you.' He was alive with excitement.

'You're the only person I want to tell!'

So Happy

In the bar, Marion curled her fingers round the chilled glass and looked at him.

'I've found my daughter!' he said, and the glass seemed to turn into a column of ice in her hands.

'Be happy for me, Marion — I was afraid this day would never come!' He beamed at her.

'After the divorce twenty years ago, Abigail went to live with her mother and her new husband here in France.

'I was working in the Middle East then, and visits were difficult. When I was transferred back home, I was so anxious to see more of her that I blew the whole thing.'

'In what way?' Harry had no idea how much Marion wanted to know how he'd dealt with that situation.

'I was desperate, and stupidly said I'd only finance her education if she came to Scotland. Well, Abby refused to keep in touch with me after that.' He gave Marion a rueful smile.

'Sorry to dump all this on you, my dear, but you're such a warm, compassionate person, otherwise I wouldn't burden you with . . .'

Marion swallowed, hoping her voice wouldn't let her down.

'You're not burdening me — far from it! I'm glad you feel you want to tell me. And so pleased you've found a happy ending!'

'Exactly!' He beamed again.

'About a year ago, my ex-wife told me Abby had moved to Paris with her husband and baby, so I decided I would have another try. And to show I really cared . . .'

'You learned French?' It was all clear now. Marion felt much better.

He nodded.

'I'd intended to come over and see her on my own, but when you told me about the trip, I couldn't resist it — you and the group would be here to pick up the pieces.'

He reached over to take Marion's hand.

'That sounds selfish, but — '

'No, no!' Marion said hurriedly. 'I can understand how you felt. The possibility of rejection — it's not easy.'

'Mm. I meant to leave my visit until the end of our stay, but once I got here I couldn't wait any longer.'

'And how did your daughter react?'

'Burst into tears at the sight of me, I'm happy to say.' He cleared his throat. 'But you know what the best bit was, Marion? Being able to speak to wee Fleur in her own language!

'All due to you, my dear!'

Perceptive

Dinner was a celebration that night. The group were thrilled to hear Harry had been speaking French with his granddaughter.

'They don't need to know any more than that,' Harry had told Marion. 'But I want an excuse for the champagne!'

As they sat over coffee later on, Harry shocked Marion to the core.

'I've always known you were grieving in some way, Marion. I recognise the signs. Maybe you'd like to talk about your husband, if it would help?'

Harry was very perceptive, much more than she'd realised. But Marion wasn't sure she was ready to tell him the truth.

'I'll talk, all right, Harry, but you may not like it.' She looked him in the eye. 'You're right that I'm grieving, and he's the cause. But not in the way you mean.

'Before he died, Bill did something I can't forgive him for . . . '

* ★ ★

'Oh, I like this!'

Susan stood in a long room at the top of a large Victorian house on Glasgow's Great Western Road.

More than a century ago, this had been the billiard room. A short passage to the rear led to a bedroom, kitchen and bathroom, probably the maid's rooms originally.

Now it was a compact flat, with its own enclosed spiral staircase leading up from the floor below. A pair of arched windows gave a clear view right across the city to the summit of Ben Lomond.

'Like the cupola up there?' Neil, too, was gazing upwards. 'Do you see the possibilities?'

The couple the flat belonged to, friends of Neil, couldn't afford a pricey interior designer, so Neil had suggested Susan for the job.

Susan couldn't stop gazing round.

'Do you really think I'm ready for this?'

'Sure. You have to jump in at the deep end some time. Why not get some experience now?'

This could never be a conventional design scheme, Susan knew. It would need ingenuity — and a long talk with the owners, to find out their ideas, their tastes, and their budget.

She'd made a careful plan of the room's dimensions, and was just beginning to get excited at the thought of how to play up these original features.

'When do your friends plan to move in?' she asked.

'Not until the end of summer, so you have all of the vacation to work on it.'

Except that I might be moving house at the time, Susan thought.

'Of course, there'll be time off when you're at the summer school, but there's no reason why you can't work on your plans there — with me.'

Susan felt a frisson of unease.

She knew perfectly well Neil had other students equally capable of undertaking this project, but he'd chosen her. She wasn't sure about the personal element in this, not sure at all.

On the other hand, once her anger at Alan's high-handed behaviour over the house sale had abated, she'd had a long hard think. And she'd made the decision not to give up her course, no matter what.

Alan had his new toy to play with — IngramAir. But she wasn't going to sit around playing second fiddle.

Two salaries would certainly help, and she felt sure once Alan realised how much designers could make, he'd put her decision into perspective pretty quickly.

She could work as a freelance from Heronsay. It might even help their relationship! Susan smiled grimly to herself.

She'd only just got home when Alan and Daniel arrived back from the island.

'Mum, it was wicked!' Daniel rushed into the living-room. 'We went up in the plane, and I can handle all the controls — well, I know them all. I just need my pilot's licence before I can actually use them.

'We saw my new school, and Dad says I'm to have the girls' room at the cottage. Dad just made it all happen!'

'Sounds like you had a good time — together.' She smiled, first at Daniel, then at Alan.

This is what you wanted, her eyes told him, what we both wanted, you and Daniel being closer to each other.

Alan smiled back, a little tentatively, she thought, but she guessed he'd expected her to blow up the moment she set eyes on him.

'That sign.' He nodded at the window. 'They jumped the gun, Susan, believe me. I asked them to hold off until I gave them the go ahead.'

'It's OK. After I calmed down, I guessed that was what must have happened.'

'Thank goodness.' He gave her a hug. 'I'm so glad! I don't want any more friction between us over this.' He drew back to look at her.

'Besides, we have a problem.'

'Oh, you mean about that artist renting the cottage? Is that a problem? I just thought it would give us a little income in the meantime.'

'Well, it will, but unfortunately she's discovered some rare flower on the very spot I wanted to build the extension. It's probably protected, so we'll have to think again about where to put the office.'

'So we'll be staying on here for a little longer? Just as well.'

Daniel came back from the kitchen with a roll in one hand and a fizzy drink in the other.

'No better time to tell you both,' Susan said. 'Guess what — I have a job!'

'Doing what, Mum? And do you have a mega salary?'

Susan laughed.

'I don't have any salary! It's just work experience.'

'What kind of work experience?'

Alan's tone was evenly controlled.

146

Susan heard it, but her enthusiasm made her ignore the warning sign.

A Chance For Susan

She did her best to describe the fantastic room she'd be engaged to transform, and then saw Alan's face.

'And how did you find out about this?'

'My tutor put my name forward — the flat belongs to a friend of his. It's marvellous training for me, Alan, don't you think?' She threw out the challenge.

'Training for what?'

If he wanted a showdown, Susan was ready for him.

'I'm going to be a freelance designer. Once I'm qualified, I'll be able to take on work anywhere in Scotland.'

'Once you've qualified. You'll be spending another year at college?'

'Yes,' she said calmly. 'In eighteen months, I'll be earning — two salaries coming in.'

'Great. Mum!' Daniel had computer

upgrade signs in his eyes, but Susan was looking at his father.

'But what about IngramAir? Don't you want to run the office side for me?'

'What? You've never mentioned this before!' Susan was completely taken aback.

'Didn't think I had to. I assumed you'd want to help.'

'For heaven's sake, Alan — ' Susan began, but then the phone rang.

'Hi! Just a minute.' It was one of Daniel's friends. He took the cordless phone with him as he went to his room.

'This tutor of yours is just using you, can't you see that?' Alan said as soon as they were alone.

'No, he isn't.' Susan retorted, 'he's giving me a chance. He thinks I can make it as an interior designer.

'Just one more year, Alan!' She stared at him.

'Alan, you do want me to make it, don't you? Because you're not acting like it. The reverse, in fact. I'm glad Dan's gone upstairs, because he shouldn't see you behaving like a dog in the manger!'

His face was a mixture of emotions. She got up and poured him a drink — then one for herself, which she didn't want, to give him time to think.

'How can I deny you the chance, after all you've done for the family?' he said at last. 'I just thought . . . well, I hoped that after all this time we'd at last be doing things together.

'Instead, I can't help feeling you're moving away from me . . . '

* * *

'If you were me, would you wear the plum lipstick or the black?' Kirralee held up both colours.

'Frankly? I wouldn't wear either.' Jessica grinned.

'The thing is, you're not into make-up, Jez. I mean — you don't need it,' Kirralee added hurriedly. 'You look great without it!'

'Cut the flattery, Kirralee. I could do

a lot more to improve myself, but I guess I just don't have the time.'

'You're always busy going from job to job! Darting about like a dragonfly.' Kirralee struck a pose.

'Is that what you think?' Jessica began to laugh.

'Well, Steve said that, actually.'

Jessica had a sinking feeling. Did Steve Berry think she was unable to concentrate — or that she was unreliable?

She remembered what she'd said to her friend in Brisbane, about life being for living, and how she expected to have loads of boyfriends. Now she knew she wasn't that kind of person at all.

A Big Sister

They were in Kirralee's bedroom trying to decide on the younger girl's outfit and make-up for the Bush Dance in the country club the following evening.

'Or maybe you're like Dad and don't

approve of make-up!' Kirralee chattered on. 'Is it a Scottish thing or something?'

'Scottish?'

'Yeah. Dad was born in Scotland. Maybe it's in the blood.'

'No way!' Jessica laughed. 'Come on, choose a pink lipstick — better for your complexion.'

'Boring!' Kirralee sang. 'Look, this is me with Mum and Dad when I was about ten.' She passed over a framed photograph to Jessica.

Jessica had only seen Mac once, in the distance, so she was curious as she took the photograph.

Mac was handsome, smiling directly at the camera.

That smile! She felt sure she'd seen it before. There was still a haunting feeling of familiarity about his face.

'Does your big sister treat you the way you treat me?' Kirralee was trying on a denim skirt.

'Oh, no. Clare's much nicer than me. You should have her for a big sister,' Jessica said.

'You'll do,' Kirralee said lightly.

She's lonely, Jessica thought, and resolved to be more patient with her.

Once she finished at the cappuccino bar, she went over to the Bush Dance the following evening.

Kirralee was surrounded by boys and girls of her own age, so Jessica found a seat beside her mum.

'This isn't going to be the same tonight.' Norelle heaved a sigh. 'Mac's not here, and he usually plays with the band. I'll miss that — but then, I'm always a wallflower anyway!' She gave a hearty laugh.

'That makes two of us.' Jessica looked round. 'Not too many folk of my age here, either.'

'In that case, I'll have my work cut out,' a voice said behind them. Steve drew up a chair, and Jessica's stomach somersaulted.

'Steve! That's good. I thought you were in Brisbane at the races?' Norelle said.

'Drove back early.' He smiled at Jessica.

'Couldn't miss your first experience of a Bush Dance.'

Later, Jessica found it hard to remember what had happened that evening. She couldn't have told you what she ate, what the band played, not after Steve arrived. Her whole attention was focused on him, the thrill of dancing with him, singing along with the music, sharing supper.

He didn't take her home, though, and he gave no indication that the evening had been special for him.

Kirralee's right, Jessica thought. He probably thinks I'm the here today, gone tomorrow type.

Perhaps it was just as well she had a charter job tomorrow to New South Wales. She could get her feelings in perspective there before she returned to work for Steve for that couple of weeks.

Stranded!

Next morning she took off with two passengers, plus Vic, who said he'd come along for the ride. His arm was still in plaster, and Jessica thought Emery wanted a more experienced pilot along.

She enjoyed handling this aircraft now — Emery had given her lots of flying time. Everything went smoothly, and they landed at a small airstrip near the property of one of the passengers.

'Do you mind if I slope off to Sydney this evening?' Vic asked. 'You can come along if you like?'

'Thanks all the same, but I'll just take it easy here.' She smiled at Vic, remembering riotous nights in the racecourse bar in Brisbane. 'Don't want to cramp your style.'

Besides, Jessica wanted no delays in returning to Copperhead. She was due to start work at Steve's surgery in forty-eight hours' time.

Vic wasn't around the following morning, so she phoned Emery to request permission to fly back alone.

'Sure, Jez, if you are confident, that's good enough for me,' her boss said. 'One thing, though. Just as a precaution, after all the trouble we've had with that plane, get the airstrip engineer to give it a thorough check.'

Four hours later, Jez was still pacing about the small airstrip office. The engineer had found a fault and was having trouble fixing it.

'New part, Jez — sorry. It'll have to come from Sydney — maybe take a couple of days,' he said.

Jessica phoned Emery with the bad news.

'I'll fly down in the other plane and you can come back with me, Jez, but it may be a couple of days, as the engineer says,' he said.

'But I'm helping Steve out the day after tomorrow!'

'Well, all I can suggest is a coach or a train from Sydney to Brisbane.'

'OK, I'll see what I can do.'

She checked out transport, but

there was no way she could reach Sydney this late in the day — it would be tomorrow at the earliest. That meant she was never going to get back in time, and she'd promised not to let Steve down!

She almost jumped out of her skin when the phone rang again.

'Hi, Jez,' Norelle's breezy voice said. 'Listen, Emery's been in touch, and I've got the answer to your problem.

'Mac's on his way home by car, but he can make a little detour and pick you up first thing in the morning.'

'Oh, Norelle, thanks!' Jessica breathed.

'It's a long drive, but you should make it back in time to be at Steve's tomorrow morning. You can sleep in the car as you go. Mac's not exactly a chatter-box, and he'll probably play music all the way home anyway.'

At dawn next day, she saw a Landcruiser with the familiar *Mac's Trail Riding Centre* logo parked near the office.

She went outside. Waiting until he'd

got out of the car, she glanced at Kirralee's dad. As soon as he began to move towards her, the same sensation of familiarity washed over her.

'Hi, you must be Jez!' Mac held out his hand and she forced herself to grip his, not let her hand go limp, although she felt her bones were melting, especially when he smiled.

She knew that smile! Subconsciously, she must have recognised it in the photograph in Kirralee's room.

Now she knew where she had seen him before — in another photograph, the one which stood on the piano at home in Scotland. The family group taken at her parents' wedding . . .

'Everyone calls me Mac around here, but my real name's Ian.' He smiled at her. 'Ready to go?'

Jessica's heart was thumping. Of course his name was Ian. But how could she tell him this meeting had turned her life upside down?

And how was she going to tell Gran?

Jessica In Shock

'Sling your gear in the back, Jez,' Mac said, and Jessica did so. Whether it was due to shock or not, she couldn't speak.

'It's a long drive back to Copperhead, and you look pretty bushed. Did you get any sleep here at all?'

His voice had traces of a Scottish accent, and Jessica's heart was still thumping. She felt so drawn to him, he was being so nice to her, and she so desperately wanted to tell him that he was her Uncle Ian!

But she couldn't.

Naturally, he was older than in the wedding photograph at home, where he stood to the right of Mum, with Granny Em and Grandad alongside.

That was the last photograph she'd seen of him — until the one in Kirralee's bedroom.

She hadn't made the connection then. It was different now, with him right next to her, warm, breathing, whistling between his teeth as they hit the road.

She had no clear idea of what had happened. He'd left home and never returned . . . Mum had told her not to speak of it to Granny Em, who was still badly hurt, she said. There had been some dreadful family row.

'You don't mind if I play some music?' Mac asked her, and she jumped. 'I find it helps pass the time on a long drive.'

'That would be great.' Jessica finally managed to speak. 'I'd better try to rest, anyway. I start work at Steve's surgery tomorrow.'

'I'll keep it at lullaby level.' There was a smile in his voice.

Mac really was a nice person, though it was a relief that, just as Norelle had said, he didn't talk much. If he'd started chatting, Jessica was sure she might have blurted it all out.

'Hi, I'm your niece Jessica, nice to meet you!'

As Mum always said, she talked first

and thought later.

What if he didn't want to know who she was? She closed her eyes. Actually, it wasn't her right to tell him, not yet. She had to check with the family — with Granny Em, if possible — exactly what had happened all those years ago.

If Kirralee was now fifteen, Mac must have been in Australia for longer than that. She remembered Kirralee saying he and her mother had met in Sydney, when Norelle was nursing him after his accident. Then they'd moved to Queensland to start up the centre.

Mac might well have come to Australia before Jessica had been born!

They had a couple of stops on the way back, for snacks, and to top up their water supply. She had learned early on never to take any journey in Australia, even a simple walk, without having plenty of water.

Fortunately, Mac seemed to accept that her lack of conversation was due to tiredness. Yet, as she climbed back into the Landcruiser, Jessica's heart gave another little flip. Mac's attitude was one of easy friendship. She felt he treated her, well, as if she was family.

But then, it dawned on her, she *was* part of the family. Kirralee was her cousin — Norelle her aunt!

She longed to tell them, Kirralee had told Jessica she'd always wanted a sister. A cousin was the next best thing!

Before she left for Steve's surgery next morning she sent a brief e-mail to Clare.

Can you tell me what happened about Mum's brother? Not a word to anyone else.

Her spirits lifted the moment Steve greeted her at the surgery. He'd heard about her being stranded, and was full of praise that she'd made it back in time.

'I wouldn't have but for Mac.'

'Lucky he was around, otherwise I guess you would have attempted to walk back!' He grinned.

'I'm not quite so intrepid as you

think.' Jessica glanced at a chart on the wall, identifying all the poisonous wild creatures she hoped never to meet.

A Shoulder To Cry On

As the days passed, Jessica found she enjoyed working in the surgery. Although she wasn't involved in any treatment, she often talked to and stroked the sick or injured animals.

There was a mixture of domestic and wild animals; cattle dogs, a gorgeous cuddly possum and a very noisy cockatoo.

Her favourite, of course, was the baby wallaby she'd comforted after Steve found him abandoned.

Well enough now to be released back into the wild, Wally was reluctant to leave.

There had been no reply from Clare, so Jessica had phoned home. Mum told her that Clare was on

Heronsay with her old school friend, Laurie.

'She left her laptop behind, but I can pass on a message, if you like?'

'It's OK, Mum. Just girl talk.'

Mum had just laughed.

Norelle had offered Jessica a room at the riding centre for this fortnight. But since realising who Mac was, Jessica was finding it stressful being with them in the evenings. She tried to act naturally, but all the time felt she was there under false pretences.

One day, during a break at the surgery, Steve confronted her.

'You're miles away, Jez. Is it something I said or did?' He sat down beside her on the veranda.

'I was — just dreaming,' she stammered.

'I don't think so. Something's worrying you. Can't you tell me?' His face was very close to hers, and suddenly she was unable to stop the tears rising in her eyes.

'Hey, my brave Jessica, it isn't that bad?'

That was the last straw. Between feeling she was deceiving Mac and his family, and the fact Steve had just called her Jessica so tenderly, instead of the casual Jez, the tears spilled out.

When he put a tender arm round her shoulder, it should have been the best moment in her whole life. But all she felt was relief. Someone to talk to!

'It's Mac,' she finally managed to say.

'Mac?'

Haltingly, she told him what she'd discovered.

'You're absolutely sure about all this?' he asked after a moment.

'It's the same person in the photographs. Ian's called Bailie, isn't he?'

'He is.'

'The thing is, I can't say anything to them until I find out why he left home. I've been trying to contact my sister — I don't want to drop the bombshell in Mum's lap, let alone Gran's, until I know what the situation is.'

'And you're feeling guilty about staying with Mac and the girls under false pretences?'

She nodded, surprised, but glad he understood her so well.

'Pretending I'm Jez, the all-round gap year girl with no worries, no loyalties, while all the time I'm family.'

Her voice broke, and Steve's thumb stroked her shoulder comfortingly.

'Right. One step at a time.' His voice was reassuring. 'Once you know what happened all those years ago, your sister can check if your gran wants to get in touch.

'If so, begin to sound out Mac. You've got something in common — Scotland. You can ask him why he came to Australia, and if he ever wants to go back. That should give you a clue, shouldn't it?'

'I didn't think to work it out like that,' she murmured.

'You're too close to the problem.' He paused, and his voice softened.

'I wish you'd talked to me before, Jessica. I hate to see you upset.'

'I've been so worried that it's maybe

a permanent rift,' she said slowly. 'Then I *would* have to leave. I couldn't live a lie.'

He was looking at her with an expression she was unable to read.

'Hey, we can't have you leaving,' he said softly. 'You've become part of the Copperhead scene! There's a bunch of us here can't do without you.'

She couldn't find the words to answer that. It was wonderful, tender and comforting, something she couldn't have dreamed of, but it was all overshadowed by Mac.

'Let's go and eat at the country club tonight,' Steve suggested. 'You can call Scotland from there — the time difference will be just right.'

But she got the answering machine at home.

'Can you give me a call some time soon, Mum? No crisis, I just need to talk.'

And that, Jessica thought as she joined Steve at their table, was the understatement of the year.

Neil's Bombshell

There was her junction at last! Susan headed for the slip road with relief. She'd been on the motorway for ever.

Despite that, she was glad she had decided to drive down to Somerset on her own. Neil had suggested several times that they travel together, but she'd turned him down.

Alan had left two days before for Heronsay. The chopper was fully booked by Gavin's guests, and he wanted to be on hand when the building work began.

'The most urgent thing is the hangar,' he told Susan. 'Then I want to talk to the architect about the cottage.'

Daniel was still away on holiday with his school friend, and Alan had taken her out to a favourite restaurant.

'To think that a tiny orchid can have such a dramatic effect!' Susan smiled ruefully at him.

'I just had to accept it.' Alan

shrugged. 'Gavin's over the moon about this book Judith is going to produce, and it will be good publicity for the island, at least.'

'At least?' Susan finished her starter. 'What does that mean?'

'Gavin's over the moon about Judith, full stop.' He refilled Susan's wine glass.

'Oh, Alan! How lovely!' Susan was delighted.

'Oh, I'm pleased for him. Time he had someone to sort him out.'

'Typical male remark! Anyway, I'll be able to see her for myself soon.'

Alan raised his eyebrows.

'I've decided not to go to Somerset,' she said. 'I'm coming to Heronsay to help you.'

Alan put his hand on top of hers.

'No, not yet. I want you to go on that course. It's important to you, and it's important to me,' he said.

'Important to you?'

'To know that I've not been completely selfish. I jumped the gun, Sue, assuming you would help. I didn't even consult you.'

'I didn't consult you about the summer school, either!'

'OK, it's a draw.' Alan squeezed her hand. 'Go on the course — for me, please — and then come to Heronsay. Now that we know we want to do everything together, we can wait another week or so.'

Interested

The course was being held in an old Victorian schoolhouse set in beautiful grounds — a gift for artists and designers.

But by the second day, Susan knew it wasn't working.

No line, no colour, no imaginative flair — her work was awful. And lurking at the back of her mind was the fact that she didn't seem to care.

Neil had noticed. He suggested they walked down to the village inn that evening.

'You aren't enjoying this, Susan,' he said bluntly when they'd found a table in the garden. 'Is something bothering you?'

His eyes were searching her face, and she hesitated for a moment.

She had been so looking forward to the course, so enthusiastic — she felt she was letting him down.

'Maybe I'm not up to it. There have been some problems at home, too — '

'It's your husband, isn't it? He's been against you the whole time,' Neil interrupted.

'Well, he wasn't too keen at first.' Susan was taken by surprise.

'Oh, you've never said a word against him, but I guessed he was making it difficult for you. He can't control your life, Susan!'

She was appalled to have given Neil that impression.

'Neil — ' She was anxious to make him understand that *her* priorities had changed, but he wouldn't let her speak.

'I've tried to help, Susan. I got you

the flat commission and persuaded you to come on the course because I believe in your talent. But you know it's more than that.' He covered her hand with his.

'You need someone to care about you, to nurture your talent. You've come to mean so much to me, Susan.'

He gazed at her, his eyes dark with longing, and Susan shakily withdrew her hand, her head reeling.

How could she have been so blind to Neil's interest in her?

'Please don't say anything more. This isn't — '

Again he interrupted her.

'Maybe it's too soon for you. But you know I'll always be there for you, whenever you need me.'

It was with great relief that Susan saw more of the group wandering into the garden to join them.

That seemed a long meal. Susan couldn't wait to get back to her room and find her mobile.

'Sue! Great to hear your voice. How's

it all going — is it good?'

Alan's voice was so warm, so sincere, that she felt tears springing to her eyes.

'I made a mistake coming here. I'm not up to speed for this,' she said. 'I'm leaving in the morning.'

'Susan, are you sure?' He sounded anxious.

'Oh, yes, very sure. I'll call you from Glasgow.'

Their goodbyes were tender, and Susan felt momentarily buoyed up by his concern. She just had to tell Neil now.

Slowly, with a heavy heart, she packed. It was much better to let Neil down now — he would be less hurt than if she went on with the course for the rest of the week.

She knew she was turning her back on the chance of completing her design course at college. It would be far too awkward seeing Neil every day.

But she also knew now that only one man mattered to her — and she was going home to him.

★　★　★

'You are in danger of becoming the class swot,' Marion threatened Harry as the group set off for the Eiffel Tower. 'Can you still speak English at all?'

He laughed.

'Too true. I just want to speak French all the time, then I can chat to Fleur.' He touched her arm.

'Are you sure you don't mind me slipping off for a couple of hours every day to see her and Abigail?'

Marion just looked at him, and smiled. Harry knew she was genuinely delighted he'd been reunited with his family. He only wished she could feel the same happiness.

During a long walk along the banks of the Seine, she'd told him about her heartache.

'My son, Ian, left home twenty years ago and I've no idea where he is.'

'A family row, I take it?'

'Not an uncommon reason at the time. He threw up his university course after a year to form a band.'

Harry was silent, waiting as she sought the way to go on.

Thrown Out

Bill was furious, of course. He was proud Ian achieved a place at university, but actually he had planned his future from the time he was a small boy.

'Ian was expected to follow the family tradition, and go into his law practice.' She gave Harry a rueful glance.

'And Ian didn't want to?'

'He seemed to go along with it, although I knew he was the adventurous type at heart. We thought law would provide security, and he could have fun in his spare time.'

'So it was a shock when he changed his mind and wanted to leave home?'

'He didn't leave.' Marion's lips tightened. 'To be more accurate, he was thrown out of the house. 'Finish the course, or make your way in the world without our support,' that was what Bill told him.'

Harry guided her to a pavement café and ordered hot chocolate.

'I went along with it because I hoped Ian would change his mind and come home. Like all mothers. I wanted a secure future for him — but you can't control your children's lives.'

'Don't I know it!' He thanked the waiter. 'That's why you're so concerned about Clare.'

Marion nodded.

'She needs to decide her future on her own.'

She paused to sip her drink.

'After a year we had a card from London.

'He said he was sorry, but he'd make a rotten lawyer. He hoped we'd forgive him and keep in touch.'

Marion stared out over the river.

'There was only a P.O. box number on the card and Bill said that meant Ian didn't really want us to keep in touch.'

'He might have been moving

around,' Harry pointed out.

'That occurred to me, but Bill was ill at the time, and I didn't want to make matters worse. I kept the card, though.'

'And you tried to get in touch later?'

'Yes. Ian needed to know about his dad — but I never heard another word.'

Harry gently folded Marion's hand in his, and she smiled at him.

'I didn't let it rest there. Susan and I went down to London, did all the rounds, tried to find friends of Ian's. No luck at all.'

'He didn't contact his sister, either?'

She shook her head.

'I bitterly regret not answering his card right away. I've failed Ian — he must think we didn't want to see him again.' Her voice trembled.

'My worst thought is something might have happened to him over the years . . .'

Harry saw she was exhausted.

'Well, we can't start finding out tonight. Let's go back to the hotel.'

His heart went out to Marion,

thinking of the burden she'd carried for so long.

The rest of the week flew by. Marion returned to her bright, well-organised self, and it seemed no time at all before they were checking in at the airport to go home.

As he collected his boarding card, Harry heard a young voice call out.

'*Grandpère! C'est moi, Fleur.*'

And there was Abigail and the flying figure of his granddaughter, making straight for him.

'*Allo, ma petite!*' He caught Fleur.

'This is a very special lady.' He introduced Marion and Abby. 'Not only has she patiently taught me French, but she's become a good friend, too.'

He hoped Marion understood that. Was she blushing? He couldn't be sure.

'He's talked about you so much,' Abigail told Marion. 'I'm so grateful to you for helping with his French. It's made things so easy for Fleur. It's meant everything to be with him again.'

Once he was settled next to Marion

on the plane, Harry knew there was just one thing he had to say to her. Seeing him so happy with Abby and Fleur must be hurting.

'Will you let me help you look for Ian again?' he asked quietly.

'But what can we do? I've tried everything I could think of.'

'Then we'll try again, start right back at the beginning. There just might be some clue. And the internet wouldn't be up and running the last time, was it?

'Let me do this with you. It took years, but I didn't give up on Abigail. You don't want to give up on Ian, do you?'

Marion gazed at him with gratitude in her eyes.

'No, I don't. You've given me hope, Harry.'

'Together we can do anything,' he said, getting carried away, and she chuckled. But she also squeezed his hand, and Harry found his heart beating faster . . .

* ★ ★

'Now don't forget, I'm expecting you to look after my wife for the next couple of weeks.' Peter Ferguson grinned at Clare. 'I'll be back in time for the birth.'

Clare had taken to Pete. He was clearly devoted to Laurie, and reluctant to return to the oil rig so close to the birth.

'Oh, get away, you big softie!' Laurie affectionately punched his shoulder. 'What better hands could I be in than those of my good doctor friend?'

'Unqualified, remember,' Clare murmured.

'Knowing you, Clare Ingram, you'll have learned your textbooks backwards by now,' Laurie teased.

Clare just smiled.

'Oh, I forgot to tell you,' Laurie went on. 'Do you remember Doctor Gillies, the GP on Bradan?'

Clare nodded.

'He still comes over to Heronsay for a weekly clinic, and I said you might like to help out!' her friend said with an impish grin.

'Oh, Laurie! I hope he said he'd pass on that.'

'Not him. Said he could always do with a spare pair of hands.' Laurie got up from the table to see Peter off.

Sound Advice

Clare wandered into the living-room and gazed out over the sea, lapping the shore not many yards away.

Laurie and Peter had a picturesque cottage at the top end of Heronsay. It was peaceful here, but Clare still felt a bit like a split personality.

One half of her was keen to carry on studying, the other wondered if she was wasting her time.

To top it all, she'd left her laptop at home in Glasgow by mistake, and wasn't able to keep in touch with Will or Jessica.

She'd phoned Will from Fearchar as

soon as she'd arrived, but she still hadn't got round to contacting Jessica.

Possibly that didn't matter. Her sister's feet rarely touched the ground at the moment, it seemed.

The two girls sat up late that evening, gossiping and chatting about old friends. Clare carefully steered away any questions about her future by getting Laurie to concentrate on the baby.

During the night, she was wakened by a noise downstairs. Worried, she slipped down to the kitchen. Laurie was sitting at the table with a mug of tea in front of her.

'You OK?'

'Couldn't sleep. I'm missing my six-foot hot-water bottle,' was Laurie's lighthearted response.

Clare poured herself some tea and sat down. Despite Laurie's casual answer, Clare was suspicious. She was looking pale, and Clare instantly felt guilty. She should never have kept her up so late chatting.

She urged her friend back to bed.

'Doctor Gillies will be on Heronsay tomorrow for the clinic, so he can check you out,' she said as she tucked her in, and Laurie didn't protest.

The clinic was held in the village hall, and Dr Gillies welcomed Clare with a hearty handshake.

'I think I last saw you when you had chicken pox on holiday here,' he told Clare. 'You're looking better!'

Everyone laughed.

'That was at least sixteen years ago!' Clare protested.

'Would you mind assisting me today?' the doctor asked quietly. 'Laurie told me you're in fourth year? I just need you to hold a few hands while I give injections, and help with the odd dressing.'

Laurie was happy to wait while the clinic ran its course, and once it was over, Dr Gillies took Clare aside.

'Have you decided to specialise in any branch of medicine?'

'Not sure.' She was reluctant to tell

him of her doubts.

'Think about general practice, lassie. I've been watching you today. You're good with folk.' He stopped.

'Why are you looking like that?'

'It's just . . . well, I'm not sure about the future. I felt I was just seeing people in hospital as — cases, not real people.' She came right out with her problem.

'Oh, we've all gone through that, Clare! You wouldn't make a good doctor if you didn't have doubts at some time.'

His tone was brisk, and Clare was momentarily heartened, but she needed to think that over.

She changed the subject.

'Is Laurie OK? I'm staying with her at the moment.'

'Aye, I was going to have a word with you. Her blood pressure is up a bit, so don't let her do too much — keep an eye on her. Don't forget there's an emergency medical kit at Fearchar.

'If you're concerned, give me a ring

— I can be here so much quicker now in your father's whirlybird.'

The next couple of days were sunny, and it was easy for Clare to persuade Laurie to relax on a deckchair in the garden. She said she needed the practice at cooking, and that worked, too.

But then on the second evening they had to come in early.

'Looks like we might have a thunderstorm.' Clare urged Laurie inside, and began stacking the garden furniture. On this side of the island the wind could be fierce.

They sat down to their tea.

'I don't feel so good. Maybe I'll lie down.' Laurie pushed her food away.

Her Own Decision

Clare remembered the next few hours for long afterwards.

She checked Laurie over, and was disturbed enough by her findings to ring Eileen for the emergency kit.

It seemed to take for ever before Ruairidh arrived in the Land-Rover.

'Nasty storm, Clare. No boats out tonight.'

Her anxiety mounting, Clare decided to phone the doctor on Bradan.

He listened carefully.

'From what you've told me about her blood pressure and urine sample, I agree with you — Laurie needs to get to hospital fast. I'm worried about pre-eclampsia.

'Get your father to take her in the helicopter to Glasgow. I'll alert the hospital — you'd better go with her.'

'But I'm not qualified!' Clare protested.

'If you're right about her, lassie, there's no time to collect me.'

No time to dwell on her doubts, either. She had to get Laurie ready and pack for them both before her dad managed to land the helicopter in a field near Laurie's cottage, despite the storm.

Laurie was most reluctant to leave,

but Clare was firm.

'This is for the baby's sake.' Clare knew it was just as much for Laurie's, but her friend would never put herself first.

Only when they were finally in the air, with her father fighting the turbulence of the storm, did the enormity of her responsibility hit Clare.

Everything relied on her having made a correct diagnosis. Dr Gillies trusted her judgement, but did she trust herself?

The alternative didn't bear thinking about. It would mean that she was putting Laurie and her baby in even more danger by making them take the flight.

Anxious Hours

'We'll be fine now, Clare. We're through the worst of it — the eye of the storm is over Bradan now.'

Dad's voice was reassuring, but it was all Clare could do to stop herself from checking and rechecking that Laurie's safety belt was secure, not putting too much pressure on her.

'I'm fine,' Laurie said into her ear. 'I know I'm in safe hands. But please let Peter know where I am as soon as possible.'

Clare promised she'd do that.

The journey seemed endless to Clare, but at last they were down on the helipad and Clare was walking alongside Laurie's wheelchair into the hospital.

'Hello, there!' A young doctor shook Clare's hand. *Dr Gill Sutherland*, her identification badge read. 'What can you tell me about your patient?'

At once, Clare felt she was back on rounds in Edinburgh. She told the doctor her assessment of Laurie's condition, her concern over possible pre-eclampsia, and then handed over her precise notes.

'You know I'm a fourth-year?' she added.

'Yes, Doctor Gillies mentioned that, but he has confidence in your judgement. Thanks for the notes — I appreciate those.' Gill Sutherland smiled at her. 'You'll want to wait?'

Clare nodded, and squeezed Laurie's hand.

'I'll contact Pete right now. See you soon!'

Laurie tried to smile, but Clare could see the anxiety in her eyes.

As she was wheeled away, Clare found a phone and broke the news to Pete. She did her best to reassure him that the transfer was just a precaution, but she didn't fool him.

'I'll get the first chopper out, but it might not be until tomorrow. Give Laurie my love, and tell her I'll be with her as soon as possible.'

Back in the waiting-room, Clare found her concern for Laurie was still at agony level. It took a few minutes for her to realise that Dad had sat down beside her.

'OK?'

'Not yet,' she told him honestly. 'I still don't know if I did the right thing in bringing Laurie out.'

'You did what you thought was right.'

He gave her a clumsy hug. 'She's in the right place now, so you can stop worrying.

'I have to get back to Heronsay now — mustn't clutter up the landing pad for long. I'm taking the plane to Glasgow first thing; Mum's going to meet me there.'

As Dad's footsteps receded from the corridor, Gill Sutherland popped her head round the door.

'Can we have a chat, Miss Ingram?'

Clare never knew how her legs carried her along to the doctor's office.

'Mrs Ferguson is fine, she's stable, all's well. Another twenty-four hours and it might have been a different story.

'You were absolutely spot on with your diagnosis.'

Clare put her head in her hands and found sobs of relief racking her body.

Dr Sutherland sat quietly until she'd regained control.

'Scary, isn't it?' she said. 'Making a critical diagnosis at your stage. I've been there, too. Patients are suddenly real people, and it's even more of a responsibility when you know them personally.'

'Yes.' Clare looked up, and searched for a hankie. 'I had to face up to that — it's been troubling me for a while. But you got through that, and qualified.'

'Sure did, as you will. Doctor Gillies was right about you.' She grinned. 'As you know, it's vital to monitor Laurie, so we'll keep her in hospital until the birth. You can see her now, and I'll ring her doctor on Bradan to update him.'

Laurie was sleepy, but smiling, especially once Clare gave her Peter's message.

'Doctor Sutherland told me that I was lucky you were there for me. Thanks.'

That was all she said, but her eyes told Clare the rest.

'I'll be around until baby Ferguson makes an appearance,' she promised.

All the way to Pollokshields, Clare couldn't stop grinning. Laurie was all right, and it was thanks to her!

The house was empty. Mum wasn't back yet from Somerset, and Daniel was still away. She picked up the mail from the hall and was surprised to see a letter addressed to her with an Australian stamp. Jessica usually kept in touch by phone or e-mail.

Then Clare remembered that she'd left her laptop here, so Jess would have had to write.

With coffee to hand, she slit the envelope and took out several closely-written sheets of airmail paper.

Her coffee remained untasted as she read the letter twice.

Clare, this is Top Secret and ultra private. Keep it to yourself until you've checked out all we need to know at your end. And now sit down.

I've found our Uncle Ian!

Did Clare know any more about the situation than she did? Jessica went on. Could she find out how Granny Em felt about getting in contact? Could she send some family photographs with

Uncle Ian in them?

Clare was still sitting with the letter in her hand when she heard her mother's car draw up outside. Hastily, she stuffed it into her bag and went to open the front door.

'Clare! What a lovely surprise. I thought you'd still be on Heronsay!'

It took about an hour for them to catch up on each other's news.

'Darling, you must be exhausted after all that, and here I am keeping you talking.' Susan hugged her daughter. 'Let's get to bed. I have to be at the airport early to meet Dad. Will you be OK here on your own? Things fine again?'

Clare smiled at her. That last sentence might sound casual, but she knew what Mum was after.

'I think so,' she said. 'It's early days yet, but I'm getting things into perspective again.'

Now was not the time to raise the subject of Uncle Ian.

Breakfast was hurried, interrupted by a call from the lawyer to say he'd had a good offer for the house.

'Dad will be thrilled with this — it's far more than we thought we'd get,' her mother said.

Then the taxi arrived.

'You won't be too lonely on your own?' Susan asked as she kissed Clare goodbye.

'Don't worry, Mum. I'll probably pop down to see Gran some time.'

'Oh, but she's away again! London this time. She and her friend, Harry, have some business there, but I wasn't told what.'

No Mum and no Gran to sound out. Well, at least she could root out some family photographs for Jessica.

She'd have loved to speak to her sister, but the letter had mentioned she would be away on flying business for a couple of weeks.

Clare arrived at the hospital later to find Peter by Laurie's side.

'The doctor thinks the baby might be early, but everything's fine.' Laurie was beaming. 'Peter has taken leave to be here for the birth.'

'Have you? I couldn't offer you a bed along the road in Pollokshields? I'm rattling around in our house, and you'll need your sleep now — before the baby comes.' Clare teased.

No-one had much sleep that night. Peter was called back at three in the morning. So when the phone rang about eleven, Clare rushed to it — but it was her boyfriend Will.

She felt an overwhelming rush of love at hearing his voice, and it was clear he felt the same.

Towards the end of their talk, he asked the question she'd been expecting.

'Too right I'm finishing the course. I'm fine with it now,' she said happily.

'That's what I needed to know. Now I won't lose you!'

'There was never any danger of that.' She smiled into the phone.

When Clare arrived at the hospital in late afternoon, bearing gifts, Alexander Ferguson lay peacefully sleeping with his doting parents beaming over him.

'Will you be his godmother?' were Laurie's first words. 'I can't help feeling that things might have been very different but for you.'

'Heavens, Laurie, I know nothing about babies. You want to inflict me on your first born?'

'You'll learn!' Pete laughed.

'You are a lovely family,' she told them.

As she left the hospital, family was very much on her mind. She'd posted half a dozen photographs to Jessica, desperately hoping they might help reunite Gran with Uncle Ian.

Gran must want to see her son again, surely? Clare was hazy about why Ian had fallen out with his parents, but Gran always said how much family mattered . . .

* * *

'You know, Alan, I feel as if I'm coming home,' Susan said as the plane circled over Heronsay.

'I hope you're not just saying that to make me feel better!'

'Things are beginning to take shape in all kinds of ways,' she said.

That morning, Alan had taken his first clients from Glasgow to Inverness — IngramAir was in business. Not only that, the businessmen had been delighted with the service and wanted to sign up for regular flights.

'Right, we're going in now.'

Susan watched his hands, lean, brown and capable, totally at home with the controls.

The plane settled down on the beach, Alan switched off the engine and they were out in the fresh air and sunshine.

'I'm not happy that you've given up your course completely,' Alan remarked as they walked up the beach.

'I think it was going away to summer school that finally clarified what I really wanted. Being so far away from you all made me see things more clearly. I want to be here with you.'

She didn't mention the uncomfortable scene with Neil. Part of her wanted to tell Alan about it — she'd always been straight with him — but now wasn't the time. Their renewed closeness was so precious; she wanted nothing to threaten that.

'Doing the course was fine while you were away — after all, it was just something new. But now we've got a new venture in common, and I want to help with IngramAir.' She ran her fingers through his hair. 'I love you, Alan.'

And they kissed, with only seabirds and seals to watch them.

'I forgot to mention,' Alan said as they approached Fearchar. 'Gavin's said we can have McArthur's barn.'

'That old ruin behind the hill?' Susan was puzzled.

'It looks like an old ruin, but the walls are sound. How would you feel if we replaced one wall with glass? Fine for a studio for you — it faces north.'

'Oh, Alan, how marvellous!' Susan was thrilled.

'So you can still use your design training. And there'll be room for an office for IngramAir at the far end. I've even bought a computer, but I'll have to get Daniel to show me how to use it!'

As they laughed, Susan knew it was going to work — this would be a *family* business.

When they arrived at Fearchar, Eileen came out to greet them.

'I'm so happy to be here — and that it's going to be permanent.' Susan hugged her mother-in-law.

Eileen gave her a long look.

'Good. I'm happy that it's worked out.'

Susan was keen to meet Judith, so they set off for the cottage after a quick cup of coffee.

'Gavin'll be over there, I dare say,' Eileen said as they left. 'We always know where to find him nowadays.'

'Do you indeed!' Susan grinned at her husband.

'Judith, I'm so glad to meet you. I've been dying to see your wild flower drawings — do you think that would be OK?'

That was the right thing to say. Soon the two women were talking like old friends.

'I'll be moving out in a couple of days,' Judith remarked as they put her sketches back.

'No hurry,' Susan assured her. 'We're accepting an offer for our house, but haven't got a changeover date. I'm only here for a few days anyway — I'll have to be back in Glasgow for Daniel.'

'So there's no need for you to move out at all!' Gavin beamed at her. 'Susan and Alan can stay at Fearchar.'

'I've finished my work here, Gavin.'

From the tone of Judith's voice, Susan knew she and Alan didn't need to be here.

'Alan, can we go and have at look at McArthur's barn?'

'What was that all about?' he asked as they walked over the hill.

'Sometimes you men are completely blind! Gavin wants to keep Judith here.

You're right, he's head over heels about her.'

'Hm. And what does Judith feel about him?'

'I'm guessing she's not absolutely sure. It isn't as if she's known him very long.'

'How long does it take to fall in love?'

'According to you, it took Gavin about twenty minutes!' She laughed. 'I just think we should hold off moving into the cottage for as long as possible. That might give them a chance.'

Time To Think

'I only came here to help you tidy up.' Gavin stood with his arms folded. 'But you're packing clothes, too.'

Judith's hands trembled a little as she folded a jumper.

'It isn't fair to stay on here any longer, and I have to get back to Kirkcudbright,' she said. 'I need to be in my own studio to complete the drawings. Then there's the text — all the arrangements with the printer.'

'You could always write the text here. I said I wanted to help with that.'

'Yes, but this is a busy time for Fearchar.' She glanced at him quickly, and looked away again as she saw the hurt in his eyes.

The last thing she wanted to do was to leave, but Judith knew she had to. She now knew exactly what being swept off your feet meant. It didn't give you time to think — just feel.

She needed to get back home to think about things. And then, Gavin hadn't had time to get to know her properly. She was completely different from all the other guests who visited Fearchar. He might change his mind . . .

Suddenly his hands were on her shoulders. She shivered, but then stood perfectly still.

'You will come back?'

'Yes, of course. We have to launch the book — '

His grip tightened ever so slightly.

'It's more than that, surely, Judith?'

She was silent for a moment. She just couldn't give him the reply he wanted, but she had to say something . . .

'Gavin, please give me time to think,' she faltered, and his hands dropped away at once.

'Of course. Ring me, Judith. Just ring me . . . '

★ ★ ★

Marion gazed out of the train window, wondering if Ian had done the same twenty years ago, when he and his band had left Glasgow to make their fortunes.

Sitting beside her, Harry had dozed off. She glanced affectionately at him. Without Harry she'd never have got this far.

'The boys probably made some demo tapes, at least. There might be some record of those with a music company. It's worth a try.

'And we can try the other band members on the internet . . . '

Harry's cousin in Muswell Hill had offered to put them up, and from her bedroom in the house just off the Broadway, Marion looked over the city.

Her heart was beating faster. For all she knew, somewhere out there her son might be living . . .

They began the search next morning, visiting music companies who'd been around when Ian's band began.

After lunch, Marion began to flag.

'Don't give up, my dear,' Harry urged her. 'I reckon that someone will remember the name of the band — Macaloon's Marauders!'

It was late in the afternoon before they had got anywhere. Harry had come up with the idea of visiting a music magazine.

'Don't remember the band, it must have sunk without trace, but I do know someone in the trade with the name Aloon.

'Let me just check my address book.' The journalist turned to his computer. 'This guy organises music events all over the country — Jonty Aloon. Want to give him a bell?'

Marion could only stammer her thanks. Her hand was shaking so much that Harry had to make a note of the number.

'Do you want to ring him now, or leave it until tomorrow?' Harry asked as they left the office.

'Now, please!' Marion was clinging to this slender hope.

Harry took out his mobile, and Marion watched his face as he spoke.

'Ten o'clock tomorrow? Could you give me your address? Thanks.'

He switched off the phone.

'Mr Aloon is out of the office today, but, as you heard, he'll see us tomorrow at ten. Now, I'm taking you for a meal. Tonight we're going to relax.'

Marion tucked her hand under his arm.

'You're a brick, Harry. You've been wonderfully supportive and patient, and I'll do my best, but I can't think of anything but the latest clue — my mind's buzzing.'

But next day Marion was nothing short of elated.

News At Last

The office they were to visit seemed dingier than the rest, but there was no disputing the warmth of their welcome.

'Hi, I'm Jonty.' He opened the door to them himself, and stared at Marion.

'Am I right in thinking you're Ian Bailie's mother?'

'I've found the right person!' Marion almost hugged him. 'Indeed I am! This is Harry MacMillan.'

Jonty was tall, with a spiky haircut. He was dressed entirely in black, and had the air of a successful man.

'Coffee for three, please, Amber.' He flashed a smile at his assistant.

'Sit here, Mrs Bailie, that's a comfy one. All right there, Harry? Thanks, Amber.' He poured the coffee.

'Macaloon's Marauders — those were the days. Days it was, too — we lasted only a few months!' He stopped, suddenly aware of Marion's anxious face.

'Have you come with news of Ian?' he asked quietly

'I haven't seen Ian since he left home,' Marion said. 'We've come here because I want to see him — I want that desperately.'

Her voice broke, and Harry took her hand.

'I'm sorry to say this, but I've lost touch with him,' Jonty said blankly.

Marion was numb. They'd seemed so close suddenly — and now . . .

'I got a couple of cards from Australia — then nothing,' Jonty said.

'Australia?' Marion gasped.

'Where in Australia?' Harry asked practically.

'Sydney. When the band broke up,

Ian and I took to singing in pubs, and so on. He was really king of the keyboards — and had a great voice.'

'I remember.' Marion's eyes were far away, and after one glance, Jonty sat down and fiddled with some pens on his desk.

'I remember he told me that there had been a bust-up at home. He wanted to make it up, you know.' He held Marion's gaze. 'His money from the pubs he intended to put to a college course. He wanted to earn some qualifications before he went back to see you and his dad.'

'Why Sydney, then?' Harry and Marion exchanged a puzzled glance.

'Some guy from Oz heard us sing in the pub and offered Ian a contract. The money was great, and he planned to stay only for a year or so.

'I could have gone, too, but I'd met Kate by then — my wife — so I decided to try to find a job in the admin side of the business . . . and here I am.'

'So Ian could still be out there

— maybe with a band, maybe on his own?' Marion wondered.

'It's been a long time,' Jonty said gently. 'He might have moved on, but I reckon he'll still be in the music business somehow. Mac Bailie was the name he was singing under then.'

'I can't thank you enough, Jonty.' Marion rose from her chair. 'We've got something to work on now.

'And I'm sorry I never met you when you were all at university. I'm afraid we were rather stuffy parents — we couldn't see where Ian's real ambitions lay.'

'My parents were exactly the same.' Jonty grinned. 'Even now, I don't think they can quite believe I'm respectable and have a good business!'

He opened the door for them.

'And when you speak to Ian, tell him he still owes me a pint!'

'*When* I speak to Ian!' Marion said, as they walked out into the noise and heat of a London summer. 'Oh, if only!'

'You know what, Marion, I think you've just found another job for Jessica. She can do some research out there. You have a lot more to go on.'

'Wouldn't it be wonderful if Jessica could find out even the smallest thing about Ian?' Marion's eyes shone. 'But I mustn't hold out too much hope . . .'

Telling The Truth

Jessica Ingram felt she could almost join a circus, she was so adept at juggling jobs. Flying took first priority, but Jessica was able to take on odd shifts at the cappuccino bar, and it had been a real thrill to help Steve for two weeks. But now his receptionist was back from holiday, all she could hope for was to see him at the trail riding centre.

She'd refused to take money from Norelle for helping out there, asking for riding lessons instead.

There was still the problem of Norelle wanting her to board with them while she worked at Copperhead. And Jessica couldn't do it. At any moment she might blurt out what she knew — probably to Kirralee, but the worst thing would be accidentally telling Mac himself.

When she returned to Copperhead from two weeks of flying jobs, an e-mail from Clare told her the photos were on their way, although she hadn't managed to talk things over with either Mum or Granny Em.

Jessica biked straight over to Steve's surgery. She'd asked Clare to mail the photos there, to give her time to decide on the best approach.

Steve gave her a warm smile, which made her heart lurch ridiculously. She just hoped her face wasn't giving too much away.

He fetched the package, and sat with her while she opened it and gazed at the photographs. Clare had sent Mum and Dad's wedding picture, plus some of Mum and Uncle Ian as teenagers.

'What do you think? Is that Mac?' She passed them over to Steve.

'No question,' he said quietly. 'Are you going to tell him?'

'Yes,' Jessica said at once. 'Thank goodness! I was afraid I'd blurt it out by accident, but at last I can tell him — and leave it to him to decide what he wants to do.'

'Like me to come along with you?' Steve offered.

'Oh, Steve, there's nothing I'd like better, but until I know how — Ian — feels about it, I think it should be — well, a family thing.'

'Fair enough.' He put a hand on her shoulder. 'Mac and Norelle have been my pals for years, but some things should be private.

'I just want to be there for you.'

'Thanks,' she whispered.

He kept saying the most wonderful things — but always when she had so much else to focus on. Would they ever be able to talk about themselves — or was he just being kind because she was in an emotional crisis?

She cycled slowly over to the riding centre, heart thumping, head confused, trying to work out what to say.

And it was all for nothing, because Mac wasn't there.

'Seven horses broke out of the bar paddock overnight,' Norelle explained. 'He's ridden off to round them up.'

'We wanted to go, too,' Kirralee added, 'but Dad said they'd be pretty far away by now, and it might take too long to find them. So we have to mind the store.'

Jessica sat down, the package of photos still clutched in her hand. Suddenly she felt washed out, and Norelle was quick to see it.

'Let's have some iced tea. And your room's all ready for you.'

'Norelle.' Jessica tried to sound firm. 'I'm not sure I should be staying here — I really think I ought to go back to the Copperhead Lodge. It isn't fair . . . ' Her voice trailed off.

Norelle put the drinks on the table in front of her.

'You're not getting away that easy, Jez, not now that Mac's met you.'

'What do you mean?'

'Dad said it was so long since he'd heard a Scots accent that you made him quite homesick!' Kirralee chipped in.

Jessica's power of speech deserted her as Norelle went on.

'It's made him think about his home — in Scotland, where he grew up. I've been trying for years to get him to contact his folks, but — '

Jessica reached over and took her hand.

'There's something I want you to see,' she said urgently. 'I wanted Mac to be here, but it can't wait any longer.'

She put the envelope on the table and took out the photos.

'Come and sit beside your mum,' she told Kirralee.

First she passed over her parents' wedding photograph.

'There's Dad!' Kirralee pointed.

Norelle studied the photo for a moment and then looked up, questions in her eyes.

'Those are my parents,' Jessica said. 'Ian . . . Mac . . . is standing beside my mother, Susan, his sister. She's the bride. Their parents are the couple on the other side of Mum. I asked my sister to send out our copy of this, and there are more — '

A tear splashed on to the table. Norelle was weeping.

'His family! We've found them . . . all these years! Oh, Jessica!'

Suddenly all three were in each other's arms in the biggest hug Jessica had ever been part of.

Kirralee was the first to recover.

'Can I see the other pictures Jez?'

Tears mingled with laughter as the three women studied the odd assortment of photographs of Susan and Ian growing up.

'How did you recognise him?' Norelle asked in the end.

'From the photograph in Kirralee's

room. Mum's got the same one on the piano.'

'You didn't say anything!' Kirralee protested.

Jessica took a deep breath.

'Well, there's just one problem. Nobody ever mentions what caused the split all those years ago, in case it upsets Granny Em — that's what we call Mac's mum. And I wasn't sure whether Mac would want to know or not . . .'

'You bet he will!' Norelle's wide smile was back again.

'Well, I'm pretty certain Granny Em will, too.'

Family

'If Dad's your mother's brother, then you must be my cousin!' Kirralee gave a whoop of joy.

'And you're our niece.' Norelle took Jessica's hands. 'You're family, Jez!'

'You can see how awkward I've felt living here, knowing this, but not sure if

215

I could say anything.' Jessica was so relieved the secret was out.

'Just wait until Mac comes home! He'll be over the moon.' Norelle said.

'Mum.' Kirralee's voice had taken on a different note. 'Look!'

They turned to the window. It was pitch black outside.

'Dad would never stay out this long without letting us know. If he didn't find the horses before the light went, he'd turn for home.'

Norelle stood up, her face suddenly pale.

'Check the mobile for text messages,' she said to Kirralee. 'I'll call round and ask if anyone's seen him.'

There were no texts. Kirralee and Jessica went the rounds of the stables, but when they got back there was still no word. None of the neighbours had seen him at all that day — but these 'neighbours' had stations up to a hundred miles away!

The harrowed expressions on the faces of Norelle and Kirralee told

Jessica everything.

Mac could be anywhere — and he might be injured! Had she found her uncle only to lose him again?

Wonderful News

Norelle sat by Mac's hospital bed, both her hands holding his good one. He had two broken fingers on his other hand, but they'd mend — it was the chest infection that was keeping him in hospital.

'Back to the beginning!' Mac gave her a rueful look. 'This is how we met, when I was in hospital in Sydney.'

'You were in a far worse state then.' Norelle remembered all too well how he'd been hurt in that car crash.

Her nursing skills had helped to put him back on his feet, but she'd always thought it was the complete change of direction, from the band to setting up the riding centre, that had done the rest.

'You pulled through then,' she said firmly, 'and you'll do the same this time, only faster.'

'Why — is there something wrong at the trail centre?'

'No, love. Jez is with Kirralee, and Steve is staying overnight, just to keep an eye on the girls.'

'What, then?' Mac lay back on his pillows and gazed at her.

Norelle hesitated. She was bursting to tell him the news, but Mac was still in shock after falling into that ravine . . .

'You talked about back to the beginning.' She picked up her bag. 'That's what I want to talk about. Even further back, in fact — before our time together.'

'What are you on about, girl?'

Norelle handed him the photograph of the Ingrams' wedding.

'Susan!' He studied it, holding it in his good hand, and she noticed that his thumb moved across the figures.

'Jez sent home for this,' she

explained. 'After she saw a picture of you and Kirralee.'

'Jez! Young Jessica?' He looked confused. 'But that's my sister's wedding!'

'Jez is Susan and Alan's daughter,' Norelle told him gently. 'She thought she recognised you from the photograph back home, but she didn't want to say anything until she was absolutely certain.'

Mac stared at her. She saw the muscles in his face slacken, then contract. He was fighting tears.

'Susan! Well, Jez has told us about her mother — so she's OK . . . ' He looked up again anxiously.

'Your mother is fine.' Norelle put her hand on his. 'Jez told me her grandfather passed away some years ago.'

Mac bowed his head, and Norelle kept quiet. She'd tried from time to time over the years to encourage him to contact his family, but he'd been so sure they didn't want to know . . .

'I didn't get a chance to say sorry to

him,' Mac murmured eventually. 'I was such a big disappointment to my dad.'

'I've often thought he might have wanted to say sorry to you — for sending you away,' Norelle suggested.

Mac gave her a rueful smile.

'I really thought I was going to make a fortune, you know, make them proud of me. The car crash finished all that.'

'So you decided you were a failure instead, and refused to let them know what had happened!' Norelle remembered the arguments they'd had at the time.

'I just let time go by, and each year it became harder to do anything. And then, it took us a long time to make a success of the centre.'

Part Of The Family

'Well, now you have a second chance, if you want it.'

He looked at her sharply.

'What does that mean?'

'The reason Jez didn't tell you that

you were her uncle was because she wasn't sure whether you wanted to be part of the family again.'

'She said that?'

'And I told her of course you would!'

At last, he grinned.

'I wouldn't have survived the last sixteen years without you and your love, Norelle. It's meant everything to me.'

Norelle rolled her eyes, but her voice was full of deep affection.

'Please, spare me the sentimental stuff!'

With his good hand, Mac gently drew her head towards him for a kiss.

'Look at your face,' she said shakily. 'I'll have to wipe away those tears!'

'They're yours, too.' But he took the tissue she handed him.

'I'll phone the girls and tell them you're going to be fine.' She smiled at him.

'Will you ask Jez when she calls Scotland to give everyone my love, especially my mother? I'll speak to them soon.'

Norelle saw with relief that his face had relaxed, his eyes were clearer, and his grip on her hands stronger than ever.

★　★　★

'Mum says Dad's going to be OK!' Kirralee, phone at her ear, reported to Jessica and Steve. 'Once the antibiotics kick in, he'll be able to come home.'

'Great news!' Jessica grinned.

'Mum wants you to phone Scotland right away, Jez. Dad sends his love to everyone there, especially your gran.'

'I'll be glad to. Tell him they'll be so thrilled.'

When she hung up, Kirralee hugged them both.

'Thanks, you two. I couldn't have got through this without you! If you hadn't gone up to search, and seen the horses from the air, Steve — '

The search party had found Mac lying in a ravine. He'd actually located the stray livestock, and taken out his mobile phone to call Norelle to round them up, when a dingo appeared.

Mac had stepped back, lost his balance — and his phone — and slipped into the gully.

'All's well in the end, Kirralee.' Steve hugged her again.

'OK, girls, I have to get going — surgery in thirty minutes. I'll be back later.'

Jessica's instinct was to tell him she and Kirralee were quite capable of looking after themselves. But she stopped herself in time. After all, she loved having Steve around!

The screen door swished to behind him, and Kirralee grinned at Jessica.

'Tell me again, Jez, about my new family.'

Norelle had no brothers or sisters, and her parents had a property far in the Outback, so Kirralee rarely saw them.

'Well, there's Granny Em — she's *our* granny. Em is for Marion, but she won't mind what you call her.

'Oh, Kirralee, she is going to be so

thrilled to have another granddaughter!'

'Then there's Aunt Susan and Uncle Alan?'

'And your cousin Clare, who is very different from me. Clever, and pretty, and with such a nice nature.'

'Just like me, you mean?'

Jessica threw a cushion at her.

'Daniel's thirteen, but unless you can list all the major football players in the world, you won't be able to have a conversation with him.'

'You mean he doesn't know about horses, either?' Kirralee looked shocked to the core.

'I guess he's going to have to learn! Hey, look at the time — I have to phone home. Would you like to talk to your Aunt Susan?'

Kirralee nodded shyly.

'Come over here, then, you idiot, so we can both hear what she's saying!'

Telling Susan

'Daniel, answer the phone!' Clare yelled, her head almost inside the washing machine. How could one teenager return home from camp with so many dirty clothes? Weren't Scouts supposed to be able to look after themselves?

Her brother appeared in the kitchen carrying the phone.

'Jessica — sounds a bit wound up, so what's new?'

He handed her the phone and went back out into the garden.

Jessica must have got the family photos by now, Clare realised.

'Hi — ' was all she managed to say, before her sister went into full flood.

'Clare, it's all right — it is Uncle Ian! Wait till you hear — '

Five breathless minutes later, Clare interrupted her.

'Uncle Ian is going to be fine? It's all right to tell Granny and Mum?'

'Norelle says he's going to be perfectly OK. Clare, he sent his love,

225

especially to Granny Em.'

'Oh, Jess, isn't this just wonderful?' Clare could hardly speak for tears. 'But there's only Dan and me here at the moment.

'Dad's flying to Glasgow to take Daniel, me, Laurie and her new baby to Heronsay, and Mum's still on the island. Gran's away at the moment, but I don't know how to reach her.'

'Best leave that to Mum, anyway,' Jessica remarked. 'Could Mum phone me once you've told her? Will you ask her to do that?'

'I don't think I'm going to need to ask her!'

'Before you go, Kirralee would like to say hello.'

Clare heard whispering at the other end as Jessica handed over the phone.

The young Australian cousin was shy, but Clare somehow found all the right things to say about the family, and sent her good wishes to Uncle Ian.

'Don't believe anything my sister says

about me, by the way. I'm human really.'

And she was rewarded by an infectious giggle from Kirralee.

Self-Control

Mum had to be the first to get the news, but it took all Clare's self-control not to blurt it out to Dad when they met the following morning.

Fortunately, he and Dan had a lot to catch up on, so Clare concentrated on chatting to Laurie Ferguson and nursing baby Sandy.

Once Pete had taken his family home from Claddach, Alan drove Clare and Daniel straight to the cottage.

The front door was wide open, and the smell of paint wafted out into the garden.

Susan, wearing jeans and an old sweatshirt, spattered with paint, was delighted to see them.

'Look what I've done already! All the

bedrooms have been repainted, I'm running up some new curtains and then we'll get some rugs.

'After that I'm going to start on the barn. Has Dad told you?'

The first thing that struck Clare was the difference in her mother. The tiny frown lines on her forehead had disappeared, her smile was wider, her eyes sparkling.

For a while, Clare had thought giving up the Glasgow house was tearing her mother apart, and when she heard that Mum had given up her design course, too, she'd been really concerned.

But now she was radiating enthusiasm. Clare would have to keep her news for just a little longer. They'd need a quiet time for that.

Daniel had gone upstairs to his computer, and Dad was making some tea in the kitchen.

'I've been trying to reach Granny Em on the phone,' Clare remarked.

'She's down in London. You met Harry Macmillan, didn't you, the chap in her French group? Well, it seems they've gone off there on some kind of business. Granny didn't specify exactly what, and I didn't like to ask.' Susan smiled at her.

'Now, would you like to hear about our plans?'

'Not yet,' Clare interrupted. 'I have to talk to you and Dad.'

'Oh, I see.' Her mother's expression sobered.

'It's not about me.' Clare hastened to reassure her. 'I've got good news, but I want to tell you both together.'

'Then spill the beans.' Her father carried a tray of tea things into the living-room.

Found!

'While you were away, Mum, I went through some of your family photographs,' Clare had thought and thought about how to begin this amazing story.

'Jessica asked me to send her your wedding picture, and some more of you and your family, Mum.

'You know she's been staying with the family at the riding centre — Norelle and Kirralee and Mac?'

Her mother nodded, still bewildered.

'She felt she'd seen Mac somewhere before — '

And then the whole story tumbled out.

'Ian? She's found Ian?' Susan's voice was a whisper, and Alan put his arm round her shoulders.

Clare, unable to speak, just nodded.

'Oh, Alan!' Her mother sobbed. 'I can't believe this!'

Clare waited until Mum had calmed down a little. She still had to tell them about her uncle's accident.

'Mother! I must tell her . . . Oh, no, she's in London, and I don't have a number!'

'Now, just wait a moment.' Alan pulled her back down on to the sofa beside him. 'We have to tell her this in person. Why don't we leave a message on her answerphone at home, and say we'd like her to join us here for a few days?'

'That's a good idea,' Clare said. 'It'll be a while before you can speak to Uncle Ian anyway.'

And she explained all about the accident.

'By the time Granny Em gets here, he should be able to speak to us all.'

All Susan could do was nod, tears were streaming down her face.

Even after tea and sympathy, she still couldn't settle.

'I must phone Jessica!'

'It's the wee sma' hours in Queensland at the moment,' Alan pointed out. 'Leave it till we can catch her first thing in the morning.'

Clare picked up the tray of tea things. Her parents would want to talk about all of this on their own. She'd told them as much as she knew of Uncle Ian's time in Australia.

She decided to take Daniel down to

Fearchar to see Granny Eye and Gavin.

'Let me just get something!' Daniel shot up to his room for a moment.

'I found this bag in my room. I think it must belong to that artist who was staying in the cottage.'

'Granny Eye will send it back to her,' Clare said. 'Come on — I bet Granny Eye's been baking!'

★ ★ ★

'Well, what do you intend to do with it?' Eileen held out Judith's bag.

Gavin Lamont shrugged.

'Put it over there for now. I'll take it back to the office.'

'Oh, for goodness' sake, Gavin, it's full of sketchbooks and paintbrushes! She probably needs it.'

'She couldn't wait to get away,' he replied impassively. 'If she needed it, she'd call us, I'm sure.'

Eileen looked at the strong, handsome face, now set in rigid lines. Poor lad, he had fallen hard.

She thought back twenty years, to when Gavin had been engaged to that London girl who expected him to sell Fearchar and put the money into her company.

It had taken him a long time to get over a mercenary approach like that. But Judith was totally unlike that harpy!

'You've really never met anyone like Judith before, have you?' She said.

He shrugged.

'It took a lot of courage for that lass to come here in the first place.' Eileen went back to rolling out her pastry, while Gavin busied himself checking over the menus for the next few days.

'Fearchar is way out of Judith Paton's league.'

'What do you mean by that?' he snapped, and Eileen hid a smile.

'I mean that your guests are all fairly well off, with established careers, or businesses, or whatever. Judith, in my mind, has all the potential, but she

233

wants to achieve something in her own right.

'Maybe she doesn't realise it, but she wants to prove to you she can be successful.'

'She doesn't need to do that where I'm concerned,' he growled.

'That's what you think, not what she thinks. Frankly, I think she's as fond of you as you are of her, but she wants you to be proud of her, too.'

At last, Gavin looked at Eileen.

'You mean — give her time?'

'Exactly. Don't forget she's doing this book in her dad's memory. If she'd stayed on here because she wanted to be with you, his wishes would have been taking second place, don't you think?'

'Aye, you could be right.' Gavin rose to his feet. 'I'll send the bag back — with a letter.' He grinned at her.

'A letter guaranteed not to frighten her off, leaving the way open for a return visit.'

He went through the swing door, and

she heard him mutter.

'I won't give up.'

Happiness For Marion

'What do you make of that?' Marion Bailie turned to Harry. 'I've not heard my daughter so excited for a while.'

'Play it again, love, and I'll put your kettle on.'

'Please come to Heronsay.' Susan's voice was full of excitement. 'We've something special to celebrate — I'm not going to tell you over the phone. Alan will fly you over, so all you need to do is let us know how soon you can come.'

'Well!' Marion reached for the tea caddy. 'I can't think what it can be, but I'd really like to go and tell them our news.'

'Yes. We've put so much in motion, we should have something definite soon.' Harry agreed.

'There's just one thing.' Marion

poured water into the pot and looked at him. 'Would you like to come over with me?'

Harry looked surprised.

'I wouldn't want to intrude on your family,' he protested.

'It's probably something to do with Clare — and you have met her, after all. But I couldn't have found out so much about Ian if you hadn't been there — and I want the family to know that.'

'Well, if you're sure. The story of the island and your son-in-law's new business really intrigues me, to be honest.'

Marion lifted the phone and got Susan at the cottage.

'Of course, Mum. We'd love to meet Harry.'

'Good, because he's been such a help to me in London, and I don't want to talk about that on the phone.'

Marion had never been all that keen on flying, and when she saw the size of Alan's plane, a couple of days later at

Glasgow Airport, she was appalled. It was tiny compared to the plane they'd flown in to France.

'Just remember, Em, I've flown all over the world and I do know what I'm doing.' Alan grinned at her.

'But does the plane?' she murmured, and both men laughed.

Once they were airborne, she decided to enjoy the scene from her tiny window and block out the men's conversation. Harry was in the co-pilot's seat, and Alan was giving him a minute-by-minute description of every manoeuvre.

'OK, Em? We're just going in to land. The landing-strip's the beach!'

'Mum! At last!'

At the cottage, Marion gasped at her daughter's exuberance. Susan was positively glowing — Heronsay had obviously been the right move.

She'd miss her daughter back in Glasgow, but Marion was quietly relieved that the family seemed to be on an even keel again.

'Clare's over on Bradan, helping Doctor Gillies.' Susan told them about Laurie's new baby, and the drama that had surrounded the birth.

'She'll be back this evening — in time.'

'In time for what?' But Susan had moved on, to start showing them the work she'd done in the cottage. Then Marion had to catch up with Daniel.

She could feel a headache coming on, and it was a moment or two before she realised the others had left the living-room. She and Susan were alone.

'I have to tell you this, Susan, before the others come back. The reason Harry and I went to London was to see if we could find out anything, about Ian.' She paused. 'We think he might be in Australia, so I want Jessica to help — '

She stopped, aware that Susan's eyes were filling up.

'Oh, Mum.' Susan hugged her. 'That's why I asked you to come here.

Jess has found him!'

It was just as well that Susan's arms were supporting her. Years of worry and tension seemed to evaporate, leaving Marion limp with relief and joy.

'Where is he? How is he?' she asked when she could speak. 'He's well?'

'Mum, you've got another grand-daughter — Kirralee. She's fifteen. Norelle is her mum . . . ' Susan told her all about it.

'We'll be able to talk to him on the phone tonight,' she finished, and Marion nodded.

'Do you mind, my dear, if I go for a walk now? I think I need some time alone.'

She walked halfway up the hill behind the cottage, sat down on the turf and gazed out over the fields to the sea.

Ian was alive. Her son was well, and she would speak to him in a few hours' time.

The long years of missing him, trying

to keep going when her heart and conscience ached . . . she must put those behind her now.

She had to forgive Bill, first of all. If he hadn't barred her from trying to contact their son . . . But that was over now. The bitterness had gone.

She could look forward now, and rejoice in this new part of her family.

They must be wonderful people. Look how they had taken care of Jessica!

More composed, she walked back to the cottage and Harry. When she told him, he put his arms around her and held her close.

They didn't need words — they'd each found a missing child, and they rejoiced for one another.

Reunions

Years later, Marion still couldn't have said what they ate that evening. She couldn't eat a morsel.

Jessica had stipulated the precise time

for the call to Queensland, knowing when Ian would be rested enough to talk. It would be early morning there.

At last Susan dialled the number. Jessica was waiting at the other end, and at once Susan gave the phone to her mother.

Before she could speak, the room had cleared and she was alone, with Ian's voice in her ear.

'Mum? Is that really you?'

It was halting and tearful at first, but then the words flowed out. Marion smiled at the Australian intonation in his voice. She just loved it!

Suddenly, out of the blue, she remembered about Jonty Aloon.

'I've got a message for you, son. Jonty says you still owe him a beer.'

'How did you meet him?'

She explained about her visit to London, and there was a short silence at the other end of the line.

'You were still looking for me? That means everything to me, Mum.'

At last, reluctantly, she called Susan in

to speak to her brother, and finally, when everyone had spoken to everyone else, Alan produced two bottles of champagne.

'Let's drink to reunions!'

Everyone raised their glasses.

'You will have noticed that I said reunions — plural!' Alan grinned at his mother-in-law.

'I've booked two return flights to Brisbane. Can you think of anyone who'd like to go?'

'Oh, Dad, cut it out,' Daniel said. 'Mum and Gran'll be going!'

* * *

'The missus get away all right?'

Ruairidh, the Heronsay handyman, was helping Alan guide the plane in to its new hangar.

'Aye, fine. They'll reach Brisbane tomorrow.'

'There's a new fella waiting to see you at Fearchar,' Ruairidh told him.

'To see me? How did he get here?'

All Alan's friends and colleagues

were aware of the air taxi service, but as he'd been taking Susan and Marion to join the shuttle at Glasgow . . .

'Called me to fetch him in the boat.' Ruairidh gave a dramatic sigh. 'Long time since I've been called out to fetch someone! I think Gavin should pension off that boat.'

Alan was quietly amused at how quickly Ruairidh had abandoned his ferry. Gavin encouraged the islanders to use the helicopter for free trips to Bradan, working round the demands of Fearchar's guests.

Alan spotted the stranger before Ruairidh had even stopped the car. The man was standing outside Fearchar, arms folded.

Alan walked over to him.

'Hello, I'm Alan Ingram. I understand you want to see me?' He put a pleasant smile on his face.

The man was maybe a few years younger than himself, dark-haired, with a good strong face, set in firm lines.

'I'm Neil Drummond, Susan's tutor.'

'Oh, good to meet you!' Alan smiled, then spread his hands apologetically. 'I'm afraid Susan isn't here. She left for Australia this morning.'

'Australia?' Neil Drummond frowned. 'Has she gone to see Jessica?'

Now how could he know that? Yet Susan probably chatted to him about the children. She was so proud of them.

'So that's the reason she hasn't returned to college?' Neil asked.

'She's actually given up the course.'

'Given up?' Neil was clearly shocked. 'I can't believe that! Susan's one of the best students I've had in years. She has exceptional talent, and a most promising career in front of her.'

Alan was taken aback.

'It was her decision,' he said. 'She told me about it when she came back from summer school.'

Neil shot him a quick look, then turned his gaze to the sea.

'I was sorry that she left early.' He took a deep breath. 'I came here to persuade her to come back to college. I thought perhaps she might need some encouragement, some support.'

'I tried to make her change her mind, but — '

'Did you?'

Alan was startled by the challenge in Neil's voice. This man had come all the way from Glasgow, the hard way, by train and boat, to see Susan. Neil Drummond certainly must believe in Susan's talents.

Alan found himself driven by doubt. He'd never taken much interest in what was involved in Susan's course, and he'd underestimated her abilities.

Had she abandoned her ambitions for his sake — or simply thought he didn't care?

He remembered that loving and tender reunion when she came back from Somerset. He'd felt that was the beginning of a new life together.

But had Susan deliberately given up something precious to her — something he knew she deserved, after all those years of putting the family first?

She had to know that he did care
— he cared enough to give up
everything on Heronsay for her!

But she was far away on the other
side of the world, and it would be weeks
before they saw each other again.
Looking into Neil Drummond's eyes,
Alan knew those would be the longest
weeks of his life.

The Last Hurdle

Marion had only dozed on the last leg
of the flight, from Singapore to
Brisbane. She was too excited and
impatient to sleep. Susan had suggested
a stopover, but Marion just wanted to
see Ian again.

Customs passed in a blur. As they
emerged into the arrivals hall, Marion
was aware of her heart racing. Jessica
had promised to meet them . . .

'There she is, Mum — look!'

The waiting crowd seemed to swim

before Marion's eyes, but suddenly there was Jessica, waving enthusiastically from behind the barrier. And with her was another girl. It had to be Kirralee! Marion fought back rising tears.

'Granny Em, meet your new granddaughter!' Jessica said.

Marion opened her arms and Kirralee walked into them. They clung together for a long moment before Marion blinked away the mist from her eyes and gazed at her.

Kirralee was tallish, like Ian, slim, with sparkling brown eyes, tearful like her own, and a mass of brown hair, floating about her slender shoulders.

'Kirralee, you're so beautiful,' Marion murmured. 'You've no idea what a wonderful moment this is for me.'

'Me, too.' Kirralee's voice was trembling a little. 'Jessica says I can call you Granny Em. Is that OK?'

'Of course, my dear!' Marion turned to Susan. 'I can't believe I have such a lovely granddaughter.'

'I know I'm not in the lovely grand-daughter league, but you could at least say hello!' Jessica's perky voice chipped in.

'Thank you, love,' Marion whispered as they hugged. 'Thank you for finding him.'

Susan was talking quietly to Kirralee, who shed her shyness quickly as her aunt asked about Dad.

Then Jessica took over.

'Right, we'll have a coffee here, just to let you get your land legs, so to speak, and then I'm flying you down to Copperhead.'

By the time Jessica had organised drinks and pastries, Kirralee was chatting naturally to Marion and Aunt Susan. Marion noticed how her granddaughter used their names frequently — it was obvious the new relationships were very important to her.

'Dad's a lot better, Granny Em,' she explained, 'but the doctor wouldn't let him fly.

'Dad's so much looking forward to seeing you and Aunt Susan. Jez suggested I came out to meet you — to give you a taste of the new bit of the family.'

Marion flashed a grateful smile at Jessica.

'Last hurdle, Gran.' Jessica rose to her feet. 'Come and see my nice plane!'

'Oh, no,' Marion groaned, and the others laughed.

'She's as good a pilot as Alan, Mum.' Susan's eyes were twinkling. 'Is that yours, Jessica? This is just about the same size as Dad's new plane.'

'Gosh, he must be having fun, even if it is work!' Jessica helped her gran aboard. 'And a helicopter to play with, too!'

'I bet you can't wait to fly them,' Susan said.

'Mm.'

That was a casual response, Marion noticed. Probably Jessica was having too much fun in Australia to leave just yet, although she knew Susan hoped to bring her home with them.

On the short flight to Copperhead, Marion felt her heart racing again at the thought of being reunited with Ian. Seeing each other after so long might open old wounds — their phone conversations had steered clear of those, but now, face to face with Ian, it might be different.

'OK, folks, we're going in to land soon. Mum, we're flying over Uncle Ian's station now. See the riding centre?'

Susan craned to see out of the window. But as Jessica began the descent, Marion sat staring straight ahead. Kirralee had taken her hand, but her grandmother had no idea how tightly she was holding it.

Her thoughts and her heart were fixed on the boy she'd lost all those years ago, and the man she was about to meet . . .

Why Is He Here?

'Since you've come this far, please stay and have lunch,' Alan said to Susan's tutor.

To give Neil Drummond his due, he hesitated.

'I doubt Ruairidh will want to take the boat out again,' Alan said. 'I'm very happy to give you a lift to Bradan, if you don't mind a helicopter flight. I have to pick up my son from school. You'll be in time for the ferry.'

'Thanks. I'd appreciate that,' Neil admitted.

'Good! Come and meet my mother.' Alan led Neil into the Fearchar kitchen, and introduced him to Eileen.

'What a pity you've missed Susan!' She smiled at him. 'She's so enthusiastic about her interior design — she's ready to make over every house on the island!'

Alan let his mother lead the conversation and somehow, as always, Eileen's interest evoked Neil's life story; he was a widower, lived alone and was passionate about his job.

When Gavin joined them, he told Neil he'd used Susan's ideas over the years about the décor at Fearchar.

'Why not take Neil over to the new

studio?' Gavin suggested. 'You'd be interested to see where Susan's going to work, I'm sure.'

Lucky

'Wow! What I'd give for a place like this.' Neil stood in the barn gazing at the cool light flooding in from the glass wall. Then he looked at Alan.

'Can I make a suggestion?'

'Please.'

'Lighting — I'm thinking of those grey winter days. You need to compensate for that.'

'Can you give me a name?' Alan smiled at him. 'I wouldn't know where to start.'

Neil said he'd contact a friend.

'Susan's very lucky to have this. Did you set it up for her?'

'I thought she deserved a studio — though I admit I'd no idea that she was so talented. I wish I'd encouraged her to finish the course.'

'She could take her final year later — maybe in a couple of years, once your business is more settled,' Neil told him.

'Really? That's great! I'm not sure she knows that. Look, why don't you come back and see her once she's home again?'

The clear north light caught a fleeting expression on Neil's face.

'Maybe not. I'll keep in touch,' he said.

It wasn't till he'd flown Neil to Bradan that Alan put two and two together.

Why would anyone make the complicated journey to Heronsay on a whim? Susan was a talented student, but Alan could have bet there was another reason.

Not for the first time, he realised how lucky he was to have Susan's love.

Waiting for Daniel to come out of school, Alan felt much better.

He could hardly wait to tell Susan she could complete her course after all!

★ ★ ★

'So you're Steve!' Susan shook hands with him. The vet looked just as she imagined a typical Australian — tall, rangy, with an open, friendly grin.

'Good flight?' he asked as he loaded their luggage into his Landcruiser.

'Which one?' Susan laughed. 'I seem to have been in the air for half my life, but this last one was the best — and most exciting.' She glanced at her mother, and Steve was quick to pick up the signal.

'It isn't far to the centre,' he assured her. 'Maybe if you sat in the back with your mum and Kirralee, it would help.'

As they drove away from Copperhead's tiny landing field, Susan saw the easy familiarity with which Steve and Jessica were chatting in the front seats.

Although her mind was full of her brother, she'd noticed a few things about Jess since arriving in Australia.

There was a new maturity about her

— she wasn't scatty any more, she was focused.

And Susan hadn't missed the flush of pleasure on her face when Kirralee had pointed out Steve's vehicle, waiting to collect them from the airfield.

How she'd missed Jessica! It was one thing to feel good about letting your children spread their wings, but you had to live with the reality — you weren't going to see them nearly as often as you wanted.

Never would she let Jessica know that. Wings were for spreading, after all.

Steve turned off the road at the sign for *Mac's Trail Riding Centre*, and Susan felt her pulse quicken. Ahead lay a long, low bungalow with a veranda.

As Steve drew up, a small, slim woman stepped down from the deck and came to greet them. Blonde curly hair was neatly contained in a bandanna, and she wore a long cotton skirt and a T-shirt.

But it was her face that attracted Susan. Bright blue eyes shone from a tanned face. Her mouth was working a little nervously.

'Norelle?' Marion said, and Susan was surprised to see her mother jump down from the Landcruiser and rush towards Ian's wife. Norelle's hands clasped hers; they smiled and hugged.

'Thank you,' Marion said.

They all knew she was thanking Norelle for taking care of Ian.

'He's resting indoors — it's a bit hot today.' Norelle's eyes were tender.

'Come and meet Susan!'

Susan looked straight into her sister-in-law's eyes and saw compassion, humour and strength. Just the right person for Ian! They were grinning at each other. Susan knew she'd found a new friend.

'Come on, Mum. He's in here.'

Marion followed Norelle into the house.

'Kirralee, show Susan where to sit, wash — you know the rest. I'll be back in a minute.'

Norelle turned to Marion.

'Ian's in the bedroom, down here.'

'Norelle?' As Marion followed her, she guessed this had been planned to allow her and Ian to meet in private.

She caught Norelle's hand.

'I'd like you to be with us, please.'

'Oh, but — '

'I know, but *you've* been Ian's life since I last saw him. You'll never know how much it means to me, to know that he was cared for, that he's found such happiness.'

Then a door opened, and Ian came out.

A sob rose in Marion's throat. He looked older, of course. He was leaning on a stick, and he wasn't fully fit, she could see. But the hope and love in his face!

Ian handed his stick to Norelle, and took his mother in his arms.

He sat on the edge of the bed, Marion in a chair, and Norelle on the floor beside them.

'Now, we don't look back,' Marion said, striving to keep her voice steady.

'We can't do anything about the past, but we can with the future.

'I have my son again, plus a new daughter-in-law and a granddaughter. It's a whole new beginning, a new branch of the family. No more tears, just love and fun!'

'I should have known you'd say something like that.' Ian cleared his throat. 'You haven't changed a bit, Mum! You could always pinpoint what was important. Even when I left, you said I had the right to choose my future.'

'And you didn't do badly, did you?' Marion smiled at Norelle.

'Do I understand you've brought my pesky sister with you?' Ian tried to match her positive approach, although she could see tears weren't far away.

'You may see another side to your husband when these two get together again!' she joked to Norelle.

She wasn't wrong. Susan and Ian traded childish insults very soon, but

Marion knew they covered deep feelings. When her children were teenagers, there had been many a ruckus in the house, but they always defended each other against all comers.

So Far Away

As they all sat on the deck that evening, catching up on the missing years, Susan felt a wonderful sense of peace.

Ever since Clare had broken the news, Susan had realised she'd never grieved over losing her brother. She'd worried more about how it had affected her mother.

'So tell me more about Daniel! I never knew about him,' Ian said.

'You never knew about me, either!' Jessica pointed out.

'True, and was it a shock when I was told who you were!' he teased.

Susan saw the ease, familiarity and love with which Jessica had been accepted into Ian and Norelle's home . . .

Home! She hadn't phoned Alan!

'You can ring him from the office,' Ian said, and insisted on taking her there himself.

It would be early morning on Heronsay. She'd probably just catch him before he took Daniel to school.

'Sue!' She felt the warmth of love envelop her as she heard Alan's voice. 'You'll never know how great it is to hear you. You're at Copperhead? All's well, I'm sure!'

She quickly brought him up to date.

'But oh, Alan, though it's wonderful to be here with Ian, I miss you so much . . . ' Her voice tailed off.

'I'm glad you went, but I'm longing for you to come home,' Alan said softly. 'Oh, by the way, your tutor Neil Drummond was here.'

'Neil? Whatever was he doing on Heronsay?'

But then she heard Daniel's voice.

'Let me speak to Mum!'

Daniel wanted to tell her how cool

Bradan High School was, and she was relieved.

'Gotta go! Dad says if we don't leave now, I'll be late for school. He'll phone you back soon!'

Susan sat in the office for a few moments, thinking. She was pleased Daniel was settling in at his new school, but why had Neil gone to Heronsay?

She wished she'd told Alan why she'd cut short the summer school. She had nothing to blame herself for, but she wanted nothing to upset the delicate restoration of their relationship.

She'd have to sort it out on their next phone call. If only he wasn't so far away!

Will Is Home

'Hurry up!' Clare muttered, waiting for the shuttle passengers at Edinburgh Airport.

Her longing to be with Will again was mixed with anxiety about disappointing him. She didn't feel she could ever match Will's adventurous spirit.

She saw him at once, head and shoulders taller than the other passengers. His long strides brought him to her side in seconds.

As he swept her into his arms, she felt his love flow round her. She never knew how long they remained locked together.

'I reckon we might get into the Guinness Book of Records for the longest airport hug ever!' he murmured, and they gazed at each other.

'You can't have grown, but it seems like it.' She reached up to smooth a lock of hair from his forehead.

'You *have* grown,' he responded.

'Me? How?'

'More beautiful.'

'You've been away too long!' Clare shook her head.

'Let's head for your place,' she added. 'I filled the fridge for you. Shall we catch up over a pizza?'

On Will's ancient sofa, head on his shoulder, pizza plate beside them, Clare sighed happily.

'It's so good to have you back!'

'You had quite a summer, honey.' He kissed her hair.

'I'll say. Looking after Laurie and learning about general practice from Doctor Gillies was the best thing for me, Will — my confidence is back.

'More than that, I know now, being a doctor is the only way to spend my life.'

'I could have told you that, but you had to discover it for yourself.' He smiled at her.

'Did you find what you wanted in Africa?'

His eyes lit up as he began to tell her about his uncle's flying clinic, taking medicines and treatments to small villages.

'There's so much work to be done out there, so great a need!' He paused. 'It's general practice, in its way.'

She slipped her hand into his.

'You've guessed that's what I want to do eventually? I'm just a country girl at heart!'

'I don't want to lose you.' He held her close. 'Let's take it a step at a time. A lot can happen in the next couple of years . . . '

'Mm,' Clare agreed. 'And, by the way, I don't want to lose you, either . . . '

★   ★   ★

'There they are. Look at the telegraph wire leading to the house.' Steve was at the deck rail with Jessica. 'You can just see, between the trees at either end.'

Jessica peered into the night. Steve's arm was round her shoulder, his free hand guiding her in the right direction.

'Oh! Shapes moving!'

'Possums. Mum and three little ones, all in a line.'

Jessica saw them then, the plump shape of the mother possum, her long tail hanging down from the wire, and three

264

miniature versions behind her.

'They're like circus acrobats, balancing on the wire!' She turned to face Steve and sighed.

'I just love it here. All the space, the huge sky, the animals! Wish I didn't have to leave so soon.'

'Does your mother want you to go back with her?'

The others had all gone inside, leaving them in the dusk.

'I think she's assuming I will.'

'Are you ready for that?' he asked.

'Ready? That's exactly the right word, Steve. No, I'm not ready to leave here just yet. There's so much I haven't seen!'

'Then stay.'

Jessica held her breath for a moment, hoping for more, but the moments ticked silently by.

'I've changed since I came here,' she said. 'I used to attack life headlong and see what happened. Look what I've done here — this job, that job, anything that came along! But I don't want to be a drifter all my life.'

'Well, you won't find out much about Australia back in Scotland. Why not stay here and look round the country? Learn how it evolved, which way it's going.'

Jessica looked at him. His eyes were on her, a gleam of challenge visible from across the table.

It would break her heart most of all to leave Steve — the girl who had wanted to fall in love six times at least! Now she knew Steve was the only man she'd ever love — but he'd said nothing about how he felt . . .

'If you went to university in Brisbane, you could come back here every weekend.' His tone seemed carefully casual, but Jessica's heart rate picked up. Was that the Australian way of saying he cared?

'So you think I should do something with my life?'

'Sure thing. You're only nineteen — lots of time. You might find you want something different in a few years — or you might have found exactly what you want.'

Did that mean he'd still be around once Jessica had decided what she wanted from life? She had to take the chance!

She loved her family very much and would miss them terribly, but oh, she'd rather miss them all than miss Steve . . .

Jez's Decision

Susan had expected her mother to be tearful as they took off from Brisbane Airport, but Marion was dry-eyed, making notes on a small pad.

'Do something, Susan. Read, listen to music — don't dwell on the fact that you're leaving your daughter behind!' Marion patted her hand.

'I know, Mum. But you're leaving your son.' Susan dried her own tears.

'Oh, love, you've seen them! Ian's happy and fulfilled in his life with Norelle and Kirralee. We've repaired all the old wounds, and I'm looking to the future.'

It was good to see Mum so rejuvenated, so full of happiness.

'And Jessica's found what she wants to do,' Marion went on. 'That's great, though we'll miss the snap, crackle and pop of her personality!'

As the plane banked, they lost sight of Brisbane.

'It isn't for ever.' Marion was determined. 'I'm making out a time-table for my next visit, and Ian and Norelle will take time off so that we'll see other parts of Australia.

'Maybe one day they'll come to Scotland!'

'I've promised we'll visit Jessica every year, too.' Then a delightful thought occurred to Susan, and this time her smile was genuine.

She'd have to discuss her idea with Alan first. And they'd both have to get used to the fact Jessica was staying out in Australia.

Susan had seen her daughter was

attracted to Steve, but it hadn't occurred to her that was enough to keep her in Queensland.

A few days after her arrival at Copperhead, Jessica had shown Susan a sheaf of papers.

'These are prospectuses for university courses here in Queensland,' she said with her usual directness.

Susan took a deep breath.

'This is where you want to be?'

Jessica nodded.

'Is Steve part of this?'

Jessica turned her head and gazed out over the paddocks.

'You weren't slow to spot that. He is only *part* of it. He's given no indication I mean anything special to him.'

Susan picked up a couple of prospectuses.

''Animal Husbandry'. 'Environmental Studies'. Did he suggest those?'

'Yes, he did, but that's because he knows I feel really drawn to this country. He says I need a few years to make up my mind about what I really want from life.'

Susan felt growing admiration for Steve Berry. She had already pegged him as sensible and trustworthy, a caring person. He was older than Jessica, but there was nothing wrong with that. He had been very perceptive where her daughter was concerned — and he would never hurt her.

'I wouldn't want you to be disappointed,' Susan said, 'but this is where you want to be, so go for it, Jez.' Her eyes twinkled as she used the Bailies' nickname.

'I won't be, Mum. Steve's right — I need to prove myself to myself. I'm looking forward to this.' She picked up the papers again.

'I can work at weekends to pay towards my tuition fees, but I might need some help from you and Dad,' she added.

'I'm sure we'll manage something.'

Susan was touched, remembering how she'd worried about Jessica throughout her teenage years — she never seemed to settle to anything, studies erratic, a galaxy of friends . . . and now here was a sensible young woman!

'What's all this?' Ian said at her side. They hadn't noticed him coming out.

'Jessica's considering studying here in Queensland.'

Ian beamed.

'Good on you! Hey, Norelle, come and see this!'

Soon they were poring over the prospectuses.

'We'd love to have you live with us,' Norelle said. 'Come out and see us at weekends, Jez?'

Ian put his head in his hands.

'Oh, no, not another version of my sister trying to run my life!'

Jessica stared at him until she noticed his shoulders shaking.

When he raised his head, his smile was wide. He really wanted her to stay, Jessica realised.

'It would make me feel a lot happier, knowing she was with family,' Susan remarked.

'I'll pay my way,' Jessica said at once.

'Mucking out stables, chasing the snakes away?' Ian grinned at her.

There was affection and respect between her brother and her daughter, Susan saw. Knowing that, how could they stand in Jessica's way?

Jessica herself had taken them to the airport, and was visiting the university campus before returning to Copperhead.

During the long, tedious journey home, Susan often dozed off, but woke with an anxious feeling.

Despite frequent phone calls home, she hadn't mentioned Neil Drummond to Alan. But as soon as they were alone together, they had to talk about it.

Not only was she longing to see Alan again, but she'd missed the other children very much.

She wouldn't see her daughter till the weekend, when Clare and Will would come over from Edinburgh, but she had such a lot to catch up with now Dan was at school.

It was thrilling to think their new life on Heronsay was now taking shape.

The shuttle from Heathrow seemed to take for ever. Harry Macmillan had timed his return from France to coincide with theirs, and was waiting for them at Glasgow Airport.

But there was no sign of Alan.

'I got here early,' Harry reported, 'but I haven't seen him around. He does know your arrival time?'

'Oh, yes,' Susan said. 'He was flying Gavin down to visit Judith in Kirkcudbrightshire, then coming straight here to pick me up. I'll try the information desk . . . '

Her mother and Harry looked happy to be together again, but she guessed Marion must be exhausted, and persuaded them to grab a taxi home.

Terrible News

There was no message at the desk. Should she ring Eileen on Heronsay to check when Alan and Gavin had left? But then, it might worry his mother.

She was concerned herself now. Alan always contacted her if he was going to be late.

She decided to go along to his old company office and say hello to Brian Cooper, Alan's former boss.

'Susan! Hi. Great to see you! How's Alan getting on with the new company?'

Susan told him the situation, and at once he reached for the phone.

'Let me check with the control tower.'

Susan sat back, enjoying the coffee Brian had provided. But soon she realised his voice was sounding tense as he spoke to air traffic control.

She still wasn't prepared for what he said when he put the phone down.

'There's been some bad weather on the route Alan was taking. I'm sorry, Susan, but air traffic control have lost contact with him.'

'Keep Faith'

Susan felt cold. In all the time Alan had been flying commercially, she had hidden her fear from him. Now, here on their home ground, the very thing she dreaded had happened. He'd gone missing on a flight.

'Alan was flying from Heronsay to a landing strip in Kirkcudbrightshire, then Glasgow Airport, and from there back to the island.'

Brian's voice was matter of fact, and Susan tried to get a grip on herself.

'He landed at the airfield, and took off again for Glasgow, with an ETA of noon.'

Susan nodded.

'My plane from London was due in just after noon.'

'He was only about ten minutes into the flight when Glasgow lost contact with him. The plane disappeared from the screen.'

'Would he have found somewhere to land?'

'Oh, he'd try to find a safe landing place — we know he didn't go back to the airstrip. Everything's being done to find him —'

'Thanks, Brian — I know the procedure. It's just — it's always happened to someone else before.' Her voice broke.

'He is one of the most experienced and skilful pilots — in all types of aircraft,' he said encouragingly.

'Is there anyone you need to contact on Heronsay?'

Susan forced herself to think. She glanced at her watch. They should have been landing on Heronsay soon.

'I should call Alan's mother.'

Brian pushed the phone across his desk.

'Susan, lovely to hear from you!' Eileen answered at once. 'Was your plane late?'

'I'm still in Glasgow, Eileen. It's not very good news.'

She broke it to Alan's mum as gently as she could, and there was a horrified gasp from the other end of the line.

'Oh, no! Are you all right, Susan?'

How typical of Eileen!

'I'm with Brian Cooper, Alan's old boss. I'm trying to keep hold of things — that's what Alan would want.'

'Good lass,' Eileen said. 'Daniel will be out of school in a couple of hours. Shall I send Ruairidh to collect him?'

'Oh, I'd forgotten all about that! I seem to have lost track of time. Of course Dan needs collecting — ' She noticed Brian signing to her.

'Hold on a moment, Eileen.'

'I'll fly you over to collect Daniel. You'll feel better once you're home. I'll take you in the chopper,' Brian said.

She passed that on to her mother-in-law.

'I'll keep in touch, Eileen.'

'Please do.' Eileen's voice was sub-dued, loaded with anxiety. 'I think you should let Gavin know.'

'Was he Alan's passenger?'

'He's gone to see Judith — he planned to return with Alan tomorrow.

I'll give you her number.'

Susan wrote it down.

'Hope for the best, keep faith and say our prayers.' Eileen hung up.

Brave, positive words, but Susan knew Alan's mother was just as worried as she was herself.

She dialled Judith Paton's number, but her answering machine clicked on. She left a message, asking Gavin to contact her or Eileen.

She wanted the news broken as gently as possible. Alan and Gavin were almost like brothers.

'One Of Us'

The storm had almost blown itself out and there was a clear sky over the Solway Firth as Gavin and Judith walked along the rocky shore.

He still wasn't sure if he'd done the right thing, dropping in on the spur of the moment. Alan had readily agreed to make the detour before he met Susan, so Gavin had arranged for a hired car, and he drove straight to Judith's house.

Now that they were alone together, he couldn't find the words he wanted.

'What's the news from Fearchar?' Judith eventually broke the silence.

'Ah. Well, lots of exciting things have been happening for Susan Ingram . . . '

He brought her up to date on all that had happened, including Susan's trip to Australia.

'Oh, that's wonderful!' Judith's face lit up. 'It must be so special, having a big family in the first place, but to be all together again . . . '

Her voice trailed off, and Gavin saw his opening.

'Yes, they're very lucky. I'm alone in the world, with no family, you know, just like you.'

Judith gave him a sympathetic smile.

'It doesn't need to be like that . . . with us.' He reached for her hand.

'Judith, I can't bear to be parted from you any longer. I love you with all my heart. You know that.

'I haven't wanted to rush you into telling me how you feel, but I'm running out of hope.'

Her delicate face was flushed and her eyes clouded as she turned to face him.

'I think the world of you, Gavin, but I don't think I'd fit in at Fearchar.'

'What nonsense!' he protested, but she shook her head.

'I lead a pretty quiet life down here. I'm not that good socially; I don't have the natural confidence of your guests. I'm afraid I would let you down!'

Gavin smiled at her.

'My dear, sweet girl, I don't want you to marry Fearchar. I want you to marry me.'

'But surely the two of you go together?'

'Only because there's been nothing else in my life — until now.'

'But Fearchar's your heritage!'

He gazed at her in exasperation.

'Look, there are some nice dry rocks. Let's sit down while I convince you of one thing.

'It doesn't mean as much to me as you do. I'd give up Fearchar tomorrow if it meant I could have you in my life.'

'I couldn't let you do that.' Judith's tears spilled over. 'You *are* Fearchar — and Heronsay. The people love you, that's what I was so aware of when I was there. You couldn't desert them.'

'For you, I could.'

There was a long silence. Judith was gazing over her shoulder at the firth.

'I've got the proofs of my book. It looks good.'

Now was that as irrelevant as it sounded? Suddenly he saw where it might lead.

'That should make you very popular on the island. One of us, in fact.' He smiled at her.

'I hadn't thought of it that way.' The tension left her face. 'But the Heronsay book's first and foremost for my dad — and also for you.'

At last he saw love in her eyes, and

with a huge sigh of relief, he took her in his arms.

'My darling,' he murmured.

He'd told her the truth when he'd said he was ready to give up Fearchar for her, but he knew it would never come to that. This girl, his girl, had the strength of mind to face up to sadness and loss, and welcome a new challenge.

Back at the cottage, Gavin saw the proofs of the book and was amazed. Judith's drawings were exquisite, and the text was clear and informative.

'Judith, this is going to make you — and Heronsay, as well!' He was delighted.

They were so engrossed in each other that it was some time before they noticed the light on her answering machine.

Just listening to Susan's voice, Gavin knew at once something was wrong.

News At Last

Susan was barely conscious of the noise of the helicopter as it crossed the water to Bradan.

None of the hospitals in a wide radius had admitted casualties. Air and sea searches were still in operation.

'There are some large uninhabited tracts of land, and a lot of forest in that part of the country. Alan could have landed anywhere.'

She was glad of Brian's straight talking. Knowing what Alan faced made her feel closer to him, as if she was by his side, urging him to survive.

Brian touched down on the Bradan helipad in plenty of time for school coming out.

With a pang of anguish, mixed with love, she saw Daniel's face light up as soon as he saw her. He looked much older, taller and broader, in his new uniform.

He gave her a welcome-home hug, talking all the time, asking about the family in Queensland as they walked to the helipad.

'Dad still in the chopper?'

Susan took his arm, and they stopped.

'No, love. There's a problem. Dad's plane lost radio contact some time ago.'

'Dad's Been Found!'

As she explained, she watched the colour drain from Daniel's face.

'Remember Brian, Dad's old boss? He's taking us on to Heronsay.'

Daniel said nothing for a moment, then the words came at a rush.

'Dad's a brilliant pilot, Mum, and we heard about the storm this morning before he left. He'll have been prepared.'

His voice wavered.

'He is going to be all right, Mum, isn't he?'

'I hope so, but he'll expect us to be strong for him.'

Dan was no longer the confident teenager who'd run across to meet her.

He was shivering slightly, and her heart ached for him as they hurried him to the helicopter.

'I'll get right back, Susan,' Brian said as they landed. 'We'll keep in touch.'

By the time they reached Fearchar, Gavin had contacted Eileen.

'He and Judith are driving round to see if anyone's spotted the plane. He knows it's a long shot, but he wants to be doing something.'

Eileen was dry-eyed and calm, but her agony showed in her eyes. Both Susan and Daniel put their arms around her for a moment — three generations fearing for the safety of a son, husband, and father.

'Don't answer the phone, Dan.' Eileen broke away as it began to ring. 'It'll be the Press — the answerphone can take it.

'No doubt you're starving?'

Daniel said he wasn't hungry, but his grandmother took them through to the kitchen and began to make something, anyway.

That was Eileen's way of coping, Susan knew, but she couldn't stay in the house.

She walked down to the jetty, her brain in a whirl. She could hardly bear to think of Alan alone, hurt . . . She just wanted to hold him, and tell him how much she loved him.

'Mum!' A positive roar reached her from up the hill, and she turned round. Daniel was racing down to the jetty.

'Dad's been found! He's OK! Quick, the police are on the phone.'

Half running, half stumbling, Susan was dragged up to Fearchar.

'He landed in a field? Concussed, but not otherwise too badly injured . . . '

With a shaky hand, she managed to take down the details of the hospital Alan had been taken to. Evidently a shepherd had found him wandering in a remote valley, and contacted the emergency services.

She thanked the police officer, put the phone down and burst into tears.

Practical as ever, but also in tears, Eileen made some tea.

'I knew Dad would be OK.' Daniel's voice was gruff. 'He's too good a pilot to — '

Just as his voice broke, Susan enveloped him in a hug.

'Come on, son. No time for that. Let's get on to this cottage hospital on Uncle Gavin's speakerphone and find out how Dad is.'

'We've just settled him in the ward, and he's not in pain,' a reassuring voice told them. 'He's going to be all right, my dear. I'll let him know you've rung, and you can speak to him yourself in the morning.'

The relief at Fearchar made them all light-headed — and brought Daniel's appetite back. His gran hugged Susan, and went back to the kitchen, smiling for the first time in hours.

Brian Cooper rang Susan's mobile next, having heard the search had been called off.

'I was pretty sure he'd be all right

— I trusted him with my best planes for years!' He sounded happy, casual, even though Susan knew he had been genuinely worried.

'Thank you so much, Brian. I'll never forget how supportive and helpful you've been.'

'Och, away, lassie! Tell Alan to contact me about retrieving the plane.'

Next, Susan rang Gavin on his mobile.

'Oh, thank God!' was his heartfelt response. 'I think we might be quite near that hospital . . .

'We're going to see him right now. I have to see him for myself!'

'Me, too,' Susan murmured. But by this time she could barely think or speak. Jet lag was kicking in, on top of the relief of knowing Alan was safe.

'I'm all in,' she admitted to Eileen. 'Could you ring the girls? Let them know that Mum and I are home safely? But play down Alan's accident . . . '

'Not to worry, love.' Eileen beamed

at her. 'I'll cope.'

And she turned to serve Daniel a second helping.

*   *   *

'How soon can we get married?'

Judith laughed at Gavin.

'I'll see the estate agent today, put this house on the market. Maybe I could have a week or two to deal with the proofs of my book?'

'Not an hour more! You'd better organise a wedding dress in that time, too.'

'Talk about being swept off your feet! Off you go and collect Alan.'

They'd been unable to see Alan the night before, but the doctor had said he'd probably be fit enough to travel home today.

Gavin didn't think he looked too good this morning. Alan had a couple of stitches in his forehead, and he seemed a bit shaky.

'I thought it was just your electrical system that conked out?' He tried to make light of it, and Alan managed a smile.

'I banged my head on landing, which must be why I didn't have the sense to call for help on my mobile.'

'You gave us all a fright.' Gavin helped him into his jacket.

'Susan most of all.' Alan took a deep breath as they went outside. 'I've spoken on the phone to her this morning and assured her I'm all in one piece. Sorry about spoiling your visit to Judith.'

'Apart from worrying about you, the visit wasn't spoiled!' Gavin opened the car door for him. 'Far from it. Let's get you home. Brian Cooper's going to fly us to Heronsay.'

Homecoming

Alan belted himself in and looked at his friend. 'I assume that ear-to-ear grin has nothing to do with my recovery. Do I hear the peal of wedding bells?'

'Absolutely. You'd better get rid of

those stitches. I need a best man in about a fortnight.'

'Couldn't have happened to a nicer guy — and girl.' Alan murmured. Then he put his head back and slept all the way to Glasgow.

By the time Brian's helicopter touched down on Heronsay, Daniel had returned from school and was at the helipad with Susan.

'Dad!' He ran to Alan and hugged him fiercely.

'Knew you'd make it, but I'm glad you're OK, too.'

'Sue!' Alan let him go.

Susan put her arms round her husband, and they held each other tightly for a long, long moment. They had so nearly lost each other. Gazing into each other's eyes, they gave thanks.

'How dare you come home a day late for your good dinner?' was all Eileen said to her son, but they understood each other.

'Brian says the plane isn't in bad shape,' Alan told Susan next day. 'Once it's repaired we'll be back in business again.'

If only there was some other business, Susan thought, but she'd been down that road before.

She could never ask Alan to give up flying. She'd just have to learn to live with the worry in future.

Flying was in Alan's blood, and all the children's. She had to accept that.

Red Letter Day

A year later, it was only as she noticed the date on the calendar that Susan remembered the accident. So much had happened since!

Today's date was circled in bright red — as if she might have forgotten! — and another, three days on, had a huge heart drawn around it.

As if she could have forgotten that either! She laughed to herself. Alan must have drawn the heart.

Today was the day Ian and his family, and her darling Jess, arrived from Queensland. Alan and Daniel had already left for Glasgow Airport to collect them.

'Tea in bed, Mum!' Clare breezed in with a neatly laid tray. 'And don't say you haven't time. Will and I are making breakfast, and Granny Em has gone for a walk with Harry. She's so excited, she can't eat a thing.'

Susan allowed herself a luxurious stretch. The whole family together — for the first time in twenty years. It was going to be some party!

They all went to Claddach beach to welcome Ian home.

'There they are!' Hanging on to Harry's arm, Marion positively bounced with excitement. 'That dot in the sky — that's them!'

Alan landed impeccably and soon the family was spilling out on to the sand.

Jessica was last out of the plane.

'I've got to say it. Nothing can stop me!' She walked over to her sister, holding out her hand formally.

'Doctor Ingram, I presume?'

'You idiot!' Clare laughed and cried at the same time.

Jessica hugged her, then congratulated Will, too.

Above the hubbub of reunion, Alan and Susan exchanged a glance. This had been the one person missing from their new life here on Heronsay — this lovely, joyous girl, with boundless enthusiasm for life.

How they loved her, how they missed her!

Jessica had almost completed her first year of animal husbandry in Queensland, and her happiness shone from her.

Jess's arm was round her mum as they all made their way back to Fearchar. Harry and Ian were deep in conversation, while Kirralee was getting to know Clare and Will.

Norelle kept stopping every few yards to admire yet another view of the Atlantic.

'Well, Titch.' Jessica grinned at

Daniel. 'What's this I hear about you being in the school swimming team?'

'Titch?' Daniel said in his recently broken voice. 'Give me a couple of years and I'll be looking down on you!'

'That'll be the day,' she retorted, but she could see it was true.

'Dan's going to be as tall as Dad, I think. And school's OK, isn't it, Dan?'

'Do we have to talk about school today?' Daniel went to catch his father up, and Jessica turned to her mother.

'So, old girl, how's business?'

'Pretty good for a near geriatric,' Susan retorted. 'Ingram and Lamont are reinventing Heronsay interiors!'

'I think it's great Uncle Gavin's married someone so artistic. Has she got him wearing matching socks yet?'

'Oh, no! That would spoil his image.'

Gavin and Judith were waiting for them at Fearchar's front door, and Susan smiled at the sight of them.

Judith, since her marriage, was transformed. Her face had filled out, the frown lines had disappeared and she seemed lit from within. Gavin had his arm around her shoulders, looking happy, contented and proud. Judith, halfway through her pregnancy, was blooming.

Inside, Eileen was waiting. She went straight to Ian and hugged him for a long moment. She'd known him well while Alan and Susan were courting, and felt heart-sore for Marion during the long separation.

Skilfully, Eileen herded them all into the kitchen.

'Scottish tea and scones — a perfect remedy for long flights, family reunions, and anything else you can think of!' She brewed the tea and indicated the big table, where a morning's baking awaited them, with sparkling jams and jellies.

'I hope there's some potato scones in that lot,' Ian said. 'It's the one treat I miss in Australia.'

'Did you think I wouldn't remember your favourite?' Eileen laughed.

Gavin insisted they should all see the

refurbished dining-room.

'Meet my painters and decorators!' He had an arm each round Judith and Susan.

Susan still couldn't believe how quickly she and Judith had set up a thriving business.

By the time Judith and Gavin returned from honeymoon, Susan had completely redecorated the cottage. By word of mouth on the island, the commissions had begun to come in.

Judith's book on Heronsay's flowers had made a hit, boosted by the romantic story of how she'd married the laird. Now she turned her talent to landscapes of Heronsay.

When Susan saw the first of them, she hugged Judith.

'You do realise these are the very colours for the Fearchar dining-room? These subdued heathery, rocky colours — can't you see it?'

Judith could. By this stage the two women had completed several commissions, and were branching out on to

Bradan and the mainland. Susan felt she had realised her dream.

She'd done something else, too. She'd returned to Glasgow to complete the interior decoration of the flat belonging to Neil's friends.

'You don't mind if I do it?' she'd asked Alan. 'I did make a promise, and I'd like to finish the place for them.'

'Of course not. You could ask Neil about taking your final year at the same time.'

She drew a deep breath.

'About his visit . . . ' she began, and he smiled at her tenderly.

'It was obvious he's very fond of you.'

'He told me so at the summer school, but to be honest, I think he's just lonely — I was someone close to his age, someone he could talk to. That was all it was.'

Susan heaved a sigh of relief.

'I've wanted to clear this up since you told me he'd been here, Alan. I didn't mention it at the time because — well, I didn't want anything so unimportant to spoil our reunion.'

'Was whatever happened at your summer school the reason you gave up the course, as well?'

She kissed him.

'Only in the sense that it made me realise what I really wanted, which was, and is, to be with you.'

He held her close.

'Besides,' she added, 'a diploma won't count for much if it means leaving all of you, even for a year.'

The Fearchar dining-room was stunning. The room looked larger, the natural island light was enhanced, and the colours in Judith's paintings were echoed in the curtains and chair coverings.

'Well done, sis,' Ian said, by Susan's side. 'All that drawing on the wallpaper back home did have a result after all!'

'And to think she was punished for it!' Their mother laughed.

'I was only six years old at the time.' Susan laughed. 'A child prodigy.'

The first few days passed in happy

reminiscence, giving the travellers time to recover, and the family time to unite.

Kirralee seemed happy to take part in whatever sport Daniel lined up, while Clare and Will often spent time with their friends Laurie and Pete, and baby Alexander.

Susan guessed that soon Clare would be spreading her wings.

Both new doctors had to complete their hospital work, but Clare and Will's future was likely to be working overseas in flying clinics like his uncle's.

'Clare's ideal for the job,' he joked to Alan and Susan. 'The original flying doctor!'

At the moment, Dan was talking of joining the RAF, but while that could change, he certainly wouldn't stay on Heronsay once he left school.

'The empty nest beckons,' Alan had said the other evening. 'Just the two old lovebirds left!'

The man who'd married them, old Mr Mitchell, came over from Bradan for the silver wedding service. Alan and Susan renewed their vows in the open air, with sunlight sparkling on the sea and their family around them.

The minister completed the service with two lines from Psalm 55.

Oh that I had wings like a dove! I would fly away and be at rest.

And, as if on cue, two doves left the dovecote and flew up into the sky.

Blessing

Her hand entwined with Alan's, Susan's heart was full. Yes, the children would fly away, but to be at rest meant to be happy, too — as she and Alan had discovered.

The wedding breakfast was a hilarious affair, only interrupted by a phone call from Australia.

'Steve sends his love and best wishes to everyone,' Jessica told them when she sat down again.

Susan reckoned he'd said quite a bit

more than that, from the happy flush on Jessica's face. All she wanted was for her daughters to find the happiness she'd found.

At the end of the meal, everyone joined hands round the table for the blessing. So many well-loved faces, each with a promise of happiness ahead.

That night, as Susan drew the bedroom curtains and heard behind her the familiar chink of Alan's cufflinks dropping into the tray, she paused to enjoy the glimmer in the sky that followed the late sunset here in the north.

Behind her, Alan cleared his throat.

'Er, Sue?'

She turned.

'I don't like the colour of these walls, I've decided.'

She stared at him.

'You said at the time that it was . . . well, nice!'

'It was your first interior design, and I didn't want to upset you.'

'Alan Ingram, this should be the happiest day of our lives, and you choose now — '

She stopped. Alan was grinning from ear to ear.

'Gotcha, Sue. Well, it was never going to be sweetness and light with us — it wouldn't be natural, would it? Yet we can't live without each other.' He reached for her, and switched off the light.

'Let's argue about the colour in the morning.'

Outside, the two doves returned to the dovecote, squabbling noisily, lovingly.

THE END

We do hope that you have enjoyed reading this large print book.

Did you know that all of our titles are available for purchase?

We publish a wide range of high quality large print books including:
Romances, Mysteries, Classics
General Fiction
Non Fiction and Westerns

Special interest titles available in large print are:
The Little Oxford Dictionary
Music Book, Song Book
Hymn Book, Service Book

Also available from us courtesy of Oxford University Press:
Young Readers' Dictionary
(large print edition)
Young Readers' Thesaurus
(large print edition)

For further information or a free brochure, please contact us at:
Ulverscroft Large Print Books Ltd.,
The Green, Bradgate Road, Anstey,
Leicester, LE7 7FU, England.
Tel: (00 44) **0116 236 4325**
Fax: (00 44) **0116 234 0205**

TUDOR STAR

Sara Judge

Meg Dawlish becomes companion to Lady Penelope Rich whom she loves and admires. Her mistress, unhappily married, meets the two loves of her life — Sir Philip Sidney, and Sir Charles Blount . . . Meg partakes in the excitement of the Accession Day Tilts and visits the house of the Earl of Essex . . . When Meg falls in love she has to decide whether to leave her mistress and life at court, and follow her lover to the wilds of Shropshire.

SAY IT WITH FLOWERS

Chrissie Loveday

Daisy Jones has abandoned her hectic London life for a more peaceful existence in her old home town. Taking on a florist business is another huge gamble, but she loves it and the people she meets. Her new life brings a new love and her life looks set for happiness . . . until the complications set in. Nothing is quite what it seems and she sets off on an emotional roller coaster. Who said life in a small town is peaceful?